POWER PLAY

E.M. GAYLE

D1736130

GYPSY INK BOOKS

POWER PLAY

By
E.M. Gayle

http://emgayle.com
Eliza on Facebook: AuthorEMGayle
Eliza on Twitter: @authoremgayle
Eliza on GoodReads

To find out about new releases, free ebooks and special sales,
please Sign Up For My Newsletter at emgayle.com/news.

* * *

CHAPTER 1

"*M*esmerizing, is it not?"

Jennifer Croft froze at the distinct lilt of the devil's voice behind her. Her core clenched. He might not have red horns and carry a pitchfork, but Daegan MacKenna was every inch the kind of man that normally sent her running in the opposite direction. At least that's what she kept trying to tell herself. Someone like him knew how to lure a woman to the dark side with his sexy-as-hell dark looks and a voice that carried the sound of hot sex and dangerous need. He scared the shit out of her.

"Yeah." Jennifer tightened the small silk robe that covered her nearly nude frame and did her best to ignore the ache between her thighs. She was going to have to go to the club tonight and get this situation taken care of. It wasn't like her to stare at a photograph, even a masterpiece such as this one, and get so turned on she couldn't think straight. She'd been so lost in thought Daegan had sneaked up on her without her knowledge.

"It's incredibly erotic to imagine what must be going through Eve's mind as Murphy pressed the knife to her throat. Chase is a genius to have captured such perfection on film."

Despite her good intentions, Jennifer turned and glanced at Daegan. The man was a damned compulsion. Every time he came near her, she couldn't decide whether she wanted to fall at his feet or slam a door in his face. The twisted ache in her stomach made no sense.

"Chase is definitely the best." She tried to hide the tremor in her voice and failed miserably.

Daegan's forehead crinkled, and his gaze narrowed. Jennifer couldn't shake the feeling of being prey as the predator circled before going in for the kill.

"I can easily imagine the flutter of her pulse at the hollow of her neck, or the sound of her heart racing to catch up with her wild thoughts." Daegan took a step closer. "The fear is palpable in a scene like this one."

Jennifer swallowed. More heat flared to life in her lower body. She clenched her thighs together and found herself biting the inside of her lip to keep from crying out.

Smooth move, Jennifer.

She'd momentarily forgotten about the rope tied intricately around her torso, including the strand that pressed a well-placed knot directly on top of her clit. In preparation for tonight's demonstration in the new Dark Room lounge, Murphy had called her in early for some prep work. Working for Chase and Murphy as one of their bondage models had morphed into an incredible career for her, and tonight's grand opening of their new space positioned her prominently as the premier fetish model in the Southeast. With any luck, after tonight's show, she'd be fielding offers from across the country, or even the world.

"What about you?"

Daegan's question pulled Jennifer from her wayward thoughts. "What? Me?" She had no idea what he'd said. For some reason his presence unnerved her, leaving her tongue-tied and mute.

"Everything okay?" The look of concern stamped on his face almost fooled her. Then he winked at her. That simple move finally clueing her in.

"I don't know what you mean?"

"Uh-huh." A rough finger touched her bottom lip,

tracing the path where her teeth had nibbled. "You looked like a lost little girl standing here waiting for the big bad Dom to eat you."

The sensation of a thousand butterflies taking wing erupted in Jennifer's stomach at his touch. She fought to maintain control and not jerk away from him. Men like him only saw that kind of weakness as a challenge, and that was the last thing she wanted to be to him. Something to conquer.

She managed to gently ease from his touch and take a step backward. "I've got to get to the Dark Room. Murphy will be waiting for me."

"Always running away, ye are. One of these days you'll find yourself trapped with nowhere to hide."

Jennifer bit back the sudden impulse to tell the silver-tongued devil where he could shove his predictions. She'd entered the club scene out of curiosity, not need, and while she loved some aspects of it, she wasn't about to become any man's slave, no matter how sexy he sounded. Instead she plastered a smile across her face and spoke sweetly. "Unfortunately duty calls. But I'm sure there will be plenty of women here tonight who'd be more than happy to take you up on your generous offer."

When she slid between two displays with her only

thought of escape, she found her wrist captured, halting her progress.

"You're a stubborn woman, Ms. Croft. Or maybe the word I'm looking for is feisty. Either way. I'm intrigued."

"I'm flattered, I really am..."

"Don't," he warned. "Don't tell me how you aren't interested. I don't believe you. Maybe if your skin didn't flush every time I touched it, or the amazing scent of your arousal didn't taunt me every time we speak, I'd believe you. So tell me the real reason. Maybe then we can figure out a way to move past this."

Despite her good intentions, heat flooded Jennifer's cheeks. The man was a danger to her sanity, or at least all of her good intentions. Getting involved with anyone beyond one or two play sessions was completely out of the question. Still... Her system rioted out of control at the mere thought of him taking charge. For weeks she'd avoided him as much as possible, until he'd finally cornered her one night at the fetish club when she'd been waiting for her turn at the flogging station.

He'd offered to scene with her, and for several brief minutes she'd considered it. Being at the club lowered what few inhibitions she had, and the thought of submitting to the man who'd begun to invade her dreams sounded like the perfect way to excise him from her thoughts.

Luckily, before she'd been able to open her mouth and make a colossal mistake, her name had been called and she'd been ushered into the flogging area. The rest of the night, every time she'd turned her head, he'd been there—watching. And from the bulge in his pants, she'd surmised he liked what he saw. The exhibitionist in her had preened. At the end of her session, while in a state of pain-induced euphoria, Jennifer had decided that if he offered again, she'd go home with him. She deserved one night of pleasure with him and then in the morning she'd explain the deal to him. To her dismay, he'd disappeared.

That little wake-up call had served her well.

Until he'd asked her to be his—temporarily.

"Why me? I'm not exactly what anyone would call a submissive."

"Because I saw the look on your face the first time I watched a whip kiss your skin. Like it or not, you crave it." When she didn't respond, he continued. "Besides, I've discovered I have a fondness for Southern girls, and you are the sweetest I've ever tasted."

Jennifer rolled her eyes. "Does that line really work?"

Daegan laughed. A rich, lilting sound she felt like an

electric jolt to her already sensitive clit. "I'll let you know tomorrow."

He brushed a lock of her hair behind her ear, and God help her, she turned her face into his touch and inhaled. The scent of wood and soap tickled her senses. Thanks to his job, she always detected a hint of wood whenever he came near. Sometimes oak, sometimes pine or like today, cedar.

She had no earthly idea why the scent of wood made her weak in the knees, but on him she couldn't get enough. Faint warning bells sounded somewhere in the back of her mind, which she promptly ignored. A few more seconds wouldn't kill her. "What were you working on today?" She almost cringed at the new husky tone of her voice.

"I had some free time today, so I spent the day working on a personal project."

"What kind of personal project?" The rough skin of his hand abraded her jaw when she moved her head back and forth. Lost in the pleasure sensations of his touch, it took her too long to realize she'd been rubbing against him like a cat in heat. In an instant her eyes cleared, and she attempted to step back.

"No." His hand tightened on the back of her neck and drew her even closer. "Have dinner with me after the show, and I'll tell you all about my new project."

Jennifer wanted to melt in Daegan's firm hold. He made her think about things that made no sense for a woman like her. "I can't. I already have plans," she lied.

"You need discipline," he growled.

"Stop saying stuff like that. You have no idea what I need." Tears formed in her eyes that she prayed wouldn't fall.

"Stop lying." He stared at her for several long seconds more before he dropped his hand and retreated. "Remember what I said earlier. One of these days you won't be able to run, little rabbit. You'll have to stand and face your fears. We all do."

Jennifer watched her Irish devil walk away, his broad body crowding the small space. Her skin tingled where he'd held her in his grip. It took all the willpower she possessed not to rub the sensation away. The sexual frustration she'd been experiencing before she'd been so rudely interrupted had now reached epic proportions. She'd be lucky if she didn't make a scene during the live demonstration. Not that anyone in this crowd would object if she spontaneously orgasmed while hanging in suspension.

She snorted at the image. Hell, Chase and Murphy would probably give her a raise.

"There you are. C'mon darlin', we're going to be late to our own party."

Jennifer reluctantly turned toward Murphy, who'd crept up behind her. Despite the frustration drowning her, she couldn't help but smile at the man in front of her. "It's a good thing Eve will be here tonight. You look downright biteable." Head to toe tight black did that to a man. Especially one as gorgeous as her boss.

"And if she catches you eyeballing me like that, it will be Eve doing the biting. Let's finish getting you ready before Chase hunts us both down." He grabbed her hand and led her down the short hallway. "Was that Daegan you were talking to?"

"As if you didn't know."

Murphy stopped and stared at her. "Feeling feisty tonight, are we? Or are you just looking to get your ass beat?" He twirled her around and began attaching more rope to the harness he'd already tied around her chest. "Either way. I'm pretty sure Daegan can handle it."

"I don't need to be handled and especially not by him." The minute the harsh words left her mouth, Jennifer regretted them. It annoyed her to no end how much she let that man get to her. But taking it out on Murphy certainly wasn't going to help.

"I'm sor—"

Murphy jerked the rope tight, pulling her off her feet and temporarily robbing her of breath. "Don't apologize to me. I'm not the one who needs to hear it. You and Daegan have been doing this little dance for weeks now. It's been kind of amusing to watch, but enough is enough, Jennifer. It's time to either fish or cut bait."

Jennifer wanted to explode over his words. How many times had she turned Daegan down? That Murphy thought she'd meant that as some sort of foreplay with the infuriating man made her want to lash out. But she knew from experience how far she could push a man like Murphy. Considering they would soon be performing for a packed audience, she settled for grinding her teeth and thinking bad thoughts.

Take a deep breath and let it go. The words of her former therapist filtered through her brain. He'd tried to tell her she had anger management issues, and after six weeks of listening to him go on and on about her faults, she'd fired his ass and never looked back.

Hell, yeah she was angry. When it was warranted.

Fortunately, Murphy had quit talking and seemed involved in getting her tied perfectly. With each pull and tug on the rope, she lost a little bit more of her freedom. Immediately a familiar calm stole over her. She closed her eyes and focused on everything around her. The cool air brushing across her exposed body, the pretty rope pressing down on her while never breaking the skin, the scent of fresh paint mingled with the crisp aroma of the brand-new leather that covered the walls.

She imagined the reality of this room when the lights were removed and there were only other senses to rely on.

Her pussy grew hot and swollen, which was only agitated by the rope covering her clit. By the end of the demonstration she'd be needy beyond belief. That idea conjured an image of her dark-haired devil. It was always the quiet ones you needed to be afraid of. Or so she kept hearing. It didn't take a rocket scientist to see below Daegan's easygoing surface to the churning waters underneath. Every time she got near him, she heard the storm brewing in her head. The energy emanating from him never ceased to arouse her.

Curiosity reared its ugly head, and once again she wondered what he'd do with her once he had her alone. He seemed insistent on her becoming his for the duration of his job. What then? The professional image of Murphy tying her for a shoot dissipated into something entirely different. Her mind wandered, and she let the feeling overtake her. It was Daegan's big body pressed against her back as he worked the intricate knots.

"There ya go, babe. All secured." The voice drifting through her senses had a sharp undertone, a gravelly sound of arousal in it.

"Ready for the paint?"

"Yes," she panted. Anything as long as it meant he'd touch her.

"Lift your arms and be perfectly still."

Jennifer eagerly obeyed despite the pain of the rope now digging sharply into her hip. Somehow that bite transferred straight to her nipples and clit, hardening them. A soft chuckle sounded from him moments before the cold, wet brush lapped at her belly. She sucked in a breath and gritted her teeth as he began to trail the liquid over her exposed skin.

The ache between her legs nearly exploded on impact. She swore her pulse thundered through her blood and pounded through her cunt.

"Legs apart." Her overimaginative brain heard Daegan speak the order. She complied. Wet stripes were painted down one side and up the other of each of her legs only inches away from her clenching opening. The rough texture of the brush excited all of her nerve endings, setting her on a course she feared. Her muscles coiled in the beginning stages of an explosive release.

"Please," she whispered in her head.

All too soon the paint was applied and her hands were cuffed to the chains dangling from the ceiling. Her arms were pulled until she stood on the tips of her toes and her cold muscles cramped in protest at the sudden movements. Her eyes flew open.

"I'll be right back. Need to check on the crowd and make sure we're all set. I'll be in hearing range if you need anything."

Jennifer licked her lips and nodded. When the door closed behind Murphy, she retreated back to the fantasy she'd begun. This time Daegan pushed a thigh between her legs and brushed against her hot spot for a brief second, her keening cry of need slipping from her lips. He took a knee and placed his face at pussy level where he teased her with hot puffs of air directed across her quaking flesh before dragging a thick finger through her sopping folds.

In the distance she heard someone say something, and then her legs were lifted and bent behind her so they could be attached to the rigging at her wrists. Daegan disappeared from between her thighs, and her pussy squeezed in protest. Reality and fantasy swirled in her head while Murphy lifted her in place. She wasn't in a scene with Daegan. This was her job. She was about to be on display in front of every single person of influence in the industry. She'd already overheard Chase talking about how many organizations and media outlets were represented tonight.

"Last piece, Jennifer. Are you ready?"

"Yes." She pushed the word through her lips. Anything to take her mind away from its insane direction.

Murphy wrapped his hand with the long, single braid of her blonde hair and pulled. "You know the drill. The more you move, the more it will hurt. Although this crowd will appreciate any pain you experience from your predicament bondage. So let's give them a show..."

"Go ahead," she urged. She no sooner said the words than pain exploded in the tender skin under her hair. Tears sprang to her eyes and threatened to fall. Jennifer relaxed, letting the painful sensation wash over her. This was what she wanted. This distraction. The reminder of who and what she was. Daegan wanted a submissive to shape and bend to his will, and she was simply a pain slut looking for a fix.

"Open your eyes, Jennifer."

The words were whispered at her ear, Murphy's hot breath bathing her skin. She lifted her lids and blinked at the eerie glow of the black light filling the room. The Dark Room had been transformed into the sensational play space it was meant to be. People mingled in nearly every inch of the small area, and the energy and excitement rushed over her, leaving her light-headed and thrumming for more. Her pulse pounded in her ears.

And then she saw him.

The crowd parted, and there along the black wall stood her sexy Irishman. Dark hair hung loose around his broad shoulders, which framed his strong jaw perfectly. The tailored shirt and slacks he wore fit in all the right places, reminding her just how hard he felt standing against her. Despite the many men and women standing around him, his gaze was all over her, drinking in every inch of her glowing skin. All the emotion and aching need from the last hour came crashing down on her. All she could picture was him taking her. Pushing his cock between her legs where she was wet and more than ready to take him.

Instead his hot stare said it all. He wanted her, and he would have her. She didn't have a doubt in her mind it was what he thought. And for the first time in several years, a paralyzing fear seized her. What if she never survived?

CHAPTER 2

or the umpteenth time, Daegan tried to push the haunted look in Jennifer's eyes from his memory. Three hours later he still burned with the image. She'd settled a hungry gaze on him so full of need it nearly brought him to his knees, and then an alarming look of fear flashed over her. He'd started to rush to her side when he'd remembered where the hell they were and what she was doing. Not only would she not appreciate the interruption, neither would Chase. Instead he'd paced, the thin veneer of his civility barely restraining the urges inside him.

They'd all worked too hard and too long to screw up now. There'd be time after the show to pry the truth from the stubborn little vixen. Then, the demonstration had ended and she'd disappeared without a word. As the evening wore down, he'd stayed behind to nurse a pint of beer and his frustrations. In this kind of mood she needed to come to him, not the other way around. So he waited in the dark. The place where he'd pretty much stayed for the last year of his life.

Daegan took another swig of his drink and pushed the past from his mind. He wasn't here to grieve anymore. He'd done enough to last a lifetime. Instead he focused on a certain model who'd managed to get under his skin in a matter of months. There was no denying her beauty. Although he preferred her when she first arrived at the studio. Fresh, no makeup, and a pretty smile that unfortunately never quite reached her eyes. The sadness he saw there always pulled at something inside him. On the outside she came across as a carefree woman who loved her life and spent all her time getting the most out of it she could. But when she thought no one saw her, he recognized something far different.

He was about to take another pull from his beer when he heard the sound of the door creaking open. A small sliver of pale light sliced through the room. Not enough to light up the area, but more than plenty for him to see who entered. A wide grin stole over his face when familiar blonde hair poked through the door followed by the long limbs of his favorite bondage model.

She felt along the wall, probably looking for a light switch or two. Unfortunately for her, unless she'd brought one of the remote controls for the room with her, she'd be searching in the dark for a while. He on the other hand had been in the room long enough for his eyes to adjust, and the low light coming in from the door gave him plenty to see. She'd removed the braid from earlier, and her hair now fell around her shoulders and halfway down her arms. From this perspective he couldn't make out things like her eye color or see the lushness of her full lips. Instead he focused on the curve of her shoulder, the indentation of her waist, and the gentle flare of her slim hips.

She had no idea how badly he ached to explore every inch of her. But she soon would. The door finally snicked closed, and they were once again plunged into complete darkness.

"Jesus, give me a break." After a few minutes of fruitless searching for a light switch, she thrust her hands in front of her and began to feel her way inside the room. When she bumped into one of the low-lying benches, she cursed and dropped to her hands and knees. He wanted to laugh but thought better of it. No need to start their next conversation off on the wrong foot.

"Can I help you find something?"

She yelped. "What? Oh my God, Daegan is that you?"

"It is. Aye."

"What the—Why are you—You scared me half to

death." The breathless tone of her voice slid over his skin, awakening his senses.

"Sorry, love. I wasn't expecting company." Although her timing couldn't have been better. Another chance to talk to her sounded a hell of a lot better than sitting here ruminating over the past.

"I'm just trying to find my keys. I think I might have dropped them from my purse earlier." She shuffled beside him, so close he swore he felt warmth emanating from her.

"I hope you brought the remote."

Silence.

"What remote?" She hesitated. "Why?"

"Well, for one, the only way you're going to get a light on in this room is either from the remote or the outside control panel."

Daegan swore her breathing increased. He hoped she didn't have a panic attack. He wanted to spend time with her but not in that capacity.

"And for two?"

"You let the door close fully behind you. It automatically locks—"

"And we need the remote to open it," she finished.

"Aye."

"Please tell me you're pulling my leg. This is some kind of joke, right?"

Daegan reached for where he thought she stood and circled her wrist. He leaned forward and whispered, "No. I'm definitely not pulling your leg."

As much as he wanted to see her reaction, he didn't need his eyes to hear the hitch in her throat or her breath coming in short pants. What he wasn't sure about was whether it was anxiety or excitement she felt.

"Don't panic," He kept his voice calm and reassuring. "It won't take long for someone to figure out we're in here. In the meantime—"

"What? Are you crazy? Everyone is gone. I had to use my employee code to get back in the building."

"Jennifer."

She didn't answer.

"It's not a big deal. Worst-case scenario, we wait until morning when Chase comes in."

"Not a big deal?" she barked at him. "Everything is a big deal with you. Ever since you made that offer to me, it's been a big fucking deal. Every time I turn around you're there. Every time I talk to Murphy he brings you up. Even Eve and Chase have encouraged me in your direction. So don't tell me it's not a big deal, because it is a big fucking deal."

Not the least bit surprised by her outburst, Daegan wrapped his arms around her waist and pulled her onto his lap. "Okay, love. 'Tis a big deal." He brushed his hand along her back in an attempt to soothe her. "Unfortunately, it looks like you're stuck with me for the night."

"What about your cell phone? Just call Chase and ask him to get us out."

He shook his head. "Don't have it. I left it upstairs so I wouldn't be tempted to interrupt the party with work."

"Of course. Figures."

He tightened his hold around her waist. "Come on, love. Don't get cross with me. I was sitting here minding my own business when you decided to join me."

Jennifer blew out a rough breath and wriggled on his lap. Good Lord, she knew how to fire his blood. Her ire did nothing to detract his attentions. Quite the opposite. Her spitfire attitude drew him in even deeper, like a moth to flame. And her backside right against his groin teased his hard-on to the limit of what he could take. She smelled good too. Sweet and saucy was certainly a potent combination.

The fact he couldn't see her at all through the inky darkness only seemed to sharpen his other senses.

She tried to pull away, and he ignored her attempts.

"There has got to be a way out of here. I mean who puts in a door with no knobs on the inside?"

Daegan smiled. "Was that a rhetorical question?"

Her shoulders lifted in a subtle shrug.

"A mean contractor with a hell of a sadistic side. That's who creates a room like this."

He felt the moment she gave in to her fate. Her rigid body posture relaxed a fraction, and the nails digging into his thigh eased their pressure.

"I'm just tired. It's been a long day, and I was looking forward to..."

She stopped before she finished, but it didn't take long to put two and two together and deduce she'd planned on a trip to the club tonight. Probably to relieve her frustration. A wave of possessiveness rolled over him. That she'd reject his offer in favor of a scene with a stranger annoyed the hell out of him. Not to mention he was sick and tired of talking about it. He had to take action.

Daegan brushed her hair to the side, leaned down and

bit her skin, right in the curve between her neck and shoulder.

"You're not alone, you know. I had a different idea on how tonight would go."

"You thought I would say yes to becoming your play toy for the next few months?"

She sounded breathless when she said that. He liked that very much. Even better was the way she relaxed into him, her body slowly becoming compliant to his touch. Did she even notice how well she responded to him? He seriously doubted it. If she did, there'd be walls slamming into place before he got in a word edgewise. He wanted her as so much more than a simple plaything, but he'd go on letting her believe differently—for now.

This one needed him to go extra slow when it came to getting to the deep-down submission he craved. If he pushed too hard, she'd go into hiding. So he'd go slow, give her pleasure, make her beg for more, and then... A little training could go a long way.

Daegan drew back and despite the darkness, he envisioned the confused look on her face. The full kissable lips that beckoned him every time he saw her. But most of all, the look in her eyes made it clear her life was missing something fairly major. "You were going to go to Purgatory tonight and play, weren't you?"

"I don—" He placed a fingertip against her lips.

"Yes or no. I don't need an explanation, an excuse, or any other variation of a long answer. Yes or no, Jennifer."

A slow exhale brushed past his finger. "Yes."

"Good girl." He cupped her chin and lifted her face to his as if they could see each other's eyes. "You can't run this time, love." He leaned forward and pressed his lips to hers, slipping his tongue between her slightly parted lips. The simple kiss quickly intensified when he took her mouth in nothing short of possession. A floodgate in his chest burst open. He pulled her closer and poured every ounce of frustration from the last few weeks into the joining of their flesh. To his surprise, she kissed him back with a fervor equal to his own. Heat, lust, desire, want—everything he'd felt for her flowed between them. He could master her, and this was his way of letting her know it without words. Words scared her, but actions didn't seem to. So he'd spend the night giving her more than she knew she desired.

Daegan didn't hesitate to make his move. He slid his hand up her back and buried it in her hair. With more than a handful, he pulled hard, breaking the kiss and drinking in the loud gasp like music to his ears.

"Tell me what you need tonight." The whispered words between them lingered in the air.

"I can't," she whispered, pain echoing in those two words.

"Can't or won't?"

"You don't understand." The hitch in her voice attacked his resolve.

"Then help me understand. Tell me."

A quiet sob filled the space between them. "I go to the club because it's the only way I know how to erase the noise."

Daegan stilled. Not in a million years did he expect a confession like that. He'd grown so accustomed to her pithy comebacks and angry responses, the truth hit him in the chest like a wicked curveball out of left field. It was important to proceed with caution, but he had to know more. "What noise, love?" He didn't dare loosen his hold on her hair, but he couldn't resist leaning forward to nip at her chin.

"It's all noise. Everything. The constant chaos of life is relentless. I only wanted a few minutes of peace." Her voice cracked on the last word. Daegan had to fight the impulse to gather her in his arms and soothe away whatever this was. God, he had to tread carefully. If he broke the moment now, he feared there wouldn't be another.

"Jennifer, trust me for tonight. Trust me to help you."

She whimpered, the sound raising the hair on his arms. Her desire for what he offered lived so close to the surface. If only he could get her to admit it. The challenge of it intrigued him beyond anything in a very long time. He wanted—no, needed to do this.

"Just for tonight?"

"Yes. In the morning you'll be free to leave." If she truly didn't want to stay with him, there wasn't much point to pushing it beyond one night.

"Okay." Her voice trembled.

A smile pulled at the corners of Daegan's mouth. In the black darkness his other senses had heightened, and even the sound of her breathing thundered in his ears, making his cock hard. He buried his face in her hair and inhaled deeply, letting the scent of her citrus shampoo mingle with the female musk unique to her skin. With her warm and compliant in his arms, it would be so easy to bend her over a bench and fuck. The image of his cock buried in her cunt nearly drove him wild every time he imagined it. He easily imagined her wet, sucking flesh taunting him to go deeper. Daegan bit back a moan. Now that he finally had her right where he wanted her, he wasn't going to waste his time with a quick fuck. If he had his way tonight, and he was certain he would, she'd be begging for more than one night. Clearly he had a new goal, and it started right now.

He tightened his grip on her hair. "Tell me."

"What?"

"Tell me what you want. It's an easy request."

Silence stretched between them. Without sight he couldn't rely on her facial expressions to tell him what was going through her pretty little head. Instead, he'd have to feel for her body language and listen carefully to her reactions.

"Jennifer," he warned. "Do I scare you?"

"A little," she mumbled.

Daegan's heart kicked faster in his chest. Blood rushed through his veins. That soft, sexy-sweet voice turned him a little inside out. He traced his fingers up her arm and along her shoulder before releasing her head so he could use both hands to draw down the zipper of her little dress. He pushed the straps from her shoulders and pulled the fabric down her torso. His hands splayed across the warm skin of her back where he immediately noticed she'd not worn a bra. God, she was like sex on a stick.

He stroked his fingers across her breast, testing to see if she'd stop him. She didn't. He cupped the weight of each breast before he brushed the tight nipples with the pads of his thumbs. Her body jerked in his direction, followed by a low and satisfying moan. She'd yet to verbally tell him what he wanted to hear, but her body nearly screamed with her desire. Daegan blazed a trail along her rib cage, which reminded him she could stand to put on some more weight before they went too far. As rough as he liked to get, he needed her at full strength. He nudged her dress from her hips and let it fall to the floor where he imagined it pooled at her feet.

With her ass revealed, Daegan couldn't resist taking some time to explore the luscious curves. More than once his nighttime fantasies consisted solely of this spot. He traced up and down the split a few times before testing her readiness with a few quick slaps. She gasped and pressed herself closer, encouraging him to continue.

"Clasp your hands behind your back and spread your legs for me." With no hesitation, she did as he asked. Since she couldn't see his face, he let a wide smile split his lips. He left her like that for several long minutes without touching her. The only sound in the room came from her. Heavy breaths as she waited to find out what he'd do next.

"Daegan?" She sounded unsure if he still stood next to her.

"What?" he asked. One way or another she wouldn't leave this room until she told him what she wanted.

"I..." She stopped again.

"Tell me." He touched her flat stomach, feeling the muscles jerk when he did. He traced circles along the hills and valleys of her heated flesh, purposely not getting too close to her breasts and pussy. A slight tremor erupted under his hand, and he knew she wouldn't withhold much longer.

"I don't know what you want me to do," she confessed.

That small admission deserved a reward. Daegan traced the slit of her cunt, elated at the moisture already formed between her legs. He pushed two fingers between her folds and began alternately rubbing and pulling at her clit.

"Does that feel good, Jennifer?" When she didn't respond, he removed his hand.

"Yes," she breathed, barely a whisper.

He'd take that answer for now. This time he pushed two fingers to her opening and plunged them deep. She met his thrust with a loud cry and grasped his shoulders to hold on to.

"Hands," he reminded her. She immediately pulled them back, and he wrapped his arm around her waist to keep her steady. Before her body could go too far, he withdrew from her heated flesh and brought his fingers to her mouth. "Open your mouth." No sooner had he uttered the command, he pushed past her lips and across her tongue. "Lick them clean."

Her sweet little tongue went to work with vigor. In seconds, she lapped every inch of his fingers, not at all offended by her own taste. "You're very wet down there, love. For all those times you've protested against me, your body has made quite the little liar out of you hasn't it?"

"Yes."

Daegan growled. Her simple admission meant the world to him. He pulled his hand from her mouth and tightened her against his frame. He made sure to bend his knees and settle the head of his covered cock at a precise juncture between her thighs. Then he sought her lips in the darkness.

The taste of her pussy exploded in his head. Good God she tasted incredible. In an incredibly exciting move, she kissed him back. A move that drove him mad. His stomach flip-flopped, and his cock throbbed mercilessly. He wanted inside her so fucking bad he thought he might implode if that didn't happen soon. First he took the time to explore her some more. From everything he'd learned about her, he couldn't push too fast. She gave skittish a run for the money. He deepened the kiss and let his hands wander over her entire body. Then he wrapped his hands around her neck and pressed his thumbs into the hollow spot above her clavicles—she kissed him harder in response.

Thank God he'd limited her movement, because if she

touched him now, they'd both be lost. The need to be thrusting inside her, rough and wild pulled at his resolve. Instead he focused on discovering more of her. He trailed his hands down her chest and explored the soft texture of her tits and the tight sensation of her bunched nipples. The more he moved, the more he connected with her on an intimate level. Somehow he'd known from the beginning she'd get inside him too fast, but he'd been helpless to resist. The urge to claim her had punched him in the gut the minute he met her. It went beyond the pretty face and the tight body. The emotions she tried to unsuccessfully hide from him drew him like a magnet.

He captured a taut nipple between his teeth and bit down, adding pressure a little at a time. He knew the precise moment he'd hit the sweet spot for her, that perfect mixture of pleasure and pain, when her hips bucked against his cock repeatedly, seeking enough friction to get her off.

Abruptly he released her. "You're not getting what you want that easy, love." Little did she know he meant that literally as well as figuratively. He groped to his right until his hand landed on the bench that had been strategically placed in the middle of the room.

"Do you have a safe word, love?"

"Yes."

"What is it?"

"Mustang," she answered.

Of course. He reached back and grabbed her hand. "Come here," he gruffly ordered. She shuffled a few feet, obviously unsure of herself in the dark. "You're going to lean over this bench and feed your hands into the loops on the legs. I've seen you trussed to this equipment before, so you should know what to do."

"Daegan, wait."

"No." He pushed between her shoulder blades and lowered her over the leather seat.

CHAPTER 3

*U*nease gripped Jennifer's stomach at the same time fire erupted between her legs. She'd had no idea how hard this would be without her sight. She'd never once allowed someone to blindfold her, and this was much worse. She couldn't just reach up and rip a cloth from her eyes and watch her world rebalance. Absolutely nothing would take away the darkness until morning.

She took a deep breath and let her mind wander to her normal comfort zone, the place where she was in control despite what happened to her body. On autopilot as if she were at a modeling job, she pushed her hands through the leather restraints and grabbed on to the metal bars. Although no amount of previous experience stopped the tremors shaking her muscles like jelly.

Daegan's big hand cupped her pussy and pressed a finger against her clit with steady pressure that shot pleasure straight to her core. Her head buzzed with sensation.

"Do you really want to stop now?" he asked. She opened her mouth to answer and no words came out. If she said yes, it would only be another lie on top of all the other lies she'd used to try and convince them both she didn't want this.

"How do you feel, Jennifer?"

"I don't..."

He growled before she could finish.

"Yes, you do. Your legs are shaking, your pussy is dripping, and I'll bet your clit aches for me to move my hand like this." He swept his wicked fingers in a short tight circle over and over again. More pressure built. Her insides tightened in a bright coil. The orgasm she'd fought earlier climbed ever closer. Much more and she'd lose all control, becoming mindless to the pleasure.

Then he stopped as quickly as he started.

"Submission isn't about learning to overcome fear. It's simply accepting it. Fear is your body's natural response to the unknown, and it's not going away. Fear excites you, doesn't it, love?"

Oh God, she didn't want to admit it. Everything excited her. The more depraved, the better. She wasn't afraid of what he'd do to her physically. In fact, if she believed he simply wanted a physical relationship, she'd be all for it. She'd overhead Chase and Eve discussing Daegan's sadist tendencies. But this... She'd never felt this.

"I don't understand it," she admitted. He wanted the truth, and that was her truth. Nothing less and nothing more.

"Do you even want to understand it? You hide too much. You push people away. You run away like a jackrabbit if someone gets too close. You'll never get very far like that. Is that what you want?"

His words hit a nerve far too deep. She struggled with the loops around her hands as tears burned her eyes. With no small amount of time, she finally managed to free one hand and started to lift from the bench.

A hand pressed against her back, pinning her in place. Then he covered her with his warm, hard body, setting off a tingling sensation inside her despite her intentions to resist.

"You've got nowhere to go this time."

"I feel stupid, Daegan. I have no idea how to be what you want me to be. I'm not—"

"If you say you aren't submissive one more time, I will take off my belt and use it," he threatened. His hand still at her pussy squeezed, rubbing her mindless before she could respond. "I can teach you what you need to learn. You've already agreed for tonight, so you only need to answer me honestly and do as you're told. That's it. Stop trying to analyze everything I say and do. That's my job."

As an orgasm once again bubbled toward the surface, all the thoughts she'd been fighting with muddled into one big mass of confusion.

"Put your hands back in those loops and hold still." His rough demand was growled directly into her ear. He was so close the day's worth of stubble on his face scraped her cheek.

A stab of uncertainty speared through her, but she did as told. Her questions and doubts easily faded under the onslaught of lust he inspired in her. Her pulse hammered through her as she worked her way into the bindings once again. The ache in her pussy increased.

Pathetic.

Before another thought made it through her brain, Daegan slid two fingers through her lower lips and thrust into her. The shocking move brought her up on her tiptoes, and her Irish devil murmured something she didn't understand.

"It's hard to deny how much you want this with my hand getting soaked, love." His thumb slid through her cheeks and circled her anus. She whimpered. "I like wet sluts."

Jennifer sucked in a sharp breath as more heat flooded her sex. Somehow the lilt of his accent made every word out of his mouth sexy, especially the dirty ones. For the first time in her life, she actually wanted him to say it again. The darker his words, the more turned on she'd get. He curved his fingers and brushed across her G-spot, and dots filled her vision. His finger pressed against the tight opening of her rear, and she automatically pushed against him, hoping he'd press into her.

Oh God Oh God Oh God Oh God.

He sank the tip of his finger inside her, and the slight pinch tumbled her into the ultimate pleasure zone.

"Tell me you want it, love." He was pushing her to confess something she no longer had resistance to.

"I do. I want this. Please, Daegan, more," she panted.

"First tell me what you're afraid of. We're alone in the dark where no one can see you. Not even me. It's the ultimate opportunity to confess." His warm breath brushed her ear on every spoken word. They rubbed her neck and taunted her to obey him.

He'd made it abundantly clear he'd accept nothing but

the absolute truth from her. With his fingers providing the ultimate distraction, she gave in. Concentrating on everything that troubled her while he worked her body proved impossible.

"I'm afraid you'll want to keep me," she shouted blindly into the room. Jennifer's blood roared in her ears as her body clenched around him in a desperate attempt to reach the pinnacle. To keep from screaming out, she bit her lip and welcomed the taste of blood on her tongue.

With shudders racking her frame, it took several long minutes before she realized he'd ceased moving his fingers. She froze. What had she said? *Fuck.*

The sound of her heavy breathing filled the room while she grappled with getting her lungs filled with air. In and out, she sucked in more oxygen until finally her pulse began to slow to an almost normal pattern.

Then he bit her on the tender skin of her neck just below the ear. Teeth scraped, fingers thrust, and her world tilted in ten seconds flat. Her orgasm hit like a flash fire, burning bright and fast. The white-hot flash felt like a combination of shards of heated glass poking at her skin and pleasure so intense she was sure her lungs were incapable of sustaining her.

With her body in near-panic mode, a harsh blow

landed across her right buttock. Fire erupted in that spot, and thousands of pinpricks erupted along her limbs. Before she could assimilate exactly what had happened, another blow landed across the opposite cheek. Jennifer opened her mouth and screamed while countless more slaps to her ass fell. Pain seared and radiated to every inch of her body. Tears pooled in her eyes.

She wanted to strangle him. *Liar.* If he stopped now, she would die. Every time his hand landed on her skin, warm pleasure pulsed through her cunt. The tremors from her release merely fed the buildup of the next one. She gripped the bars until her knuckles probably turned white. They'd certainly ache later. She began to writhe on the bench from the combination of agony and bliss.

"You're amazing, love. Only one more for tonight." The warmth spread to her belly over his compliment. She held her breath and waited. She had a feeling that if he'd decided to warn her, this last one was going to hurt like a motherfucker. And it was going to make her come.

His hand brushed her burning buttocks and soothed some of the soreness. The cotton sensation in her head expanded and unbearable pressure built behind her clit. His hand disappeared, and the last strike came swiftly. The air whooshed from her body on a wave of pain so brilliant and bright it blinded her. She bowed her back and pulled at the restraints all in an attempt for that final touch to send her soaring over the cliff.

Immediately he shifted, and his lips pressed to her burning flesh. Fingers parted her lower lips moments before he followed them with his mouth. For a fleeting second she worried about what would come next before she forced all rational thought from her mind. Instead, she focused on the slow slide of his fingers in and out of her pussy and the smooth slide of his warm tongue across her aching flesh. She'd grown so wet it was ridiculous.

"I bet you'd give anything to be fucked right about now."

She whimpered. There was no need to respond since they both knew the truth of his statement. She arched her back, opening herself for easy access to more of his ministrations. Instead Daegan pulled his fingers free and moved away.

"Don't do this, Daegan. Please, don't leave me like this." She wanted to bite down on her tongue for pleading with him but she couldn't stop. She was that desperate.

His fingers found her pussy and worked the aching bud

in a repeated circular motion. Her release grew closer with every thundering beat of her heart. The pain in her ass had developed into a dull and relentless ache, reaching everywhere he touched.

"You need me." His words were not harsh, more like reverent. They did something funny to her insides. This was the part where the heat of humiliation reared its ugly head. Needing anyone other than herself was strictly forbidden. She tried to shake her head no and found it impossible.

"You want me."

"Yes." There was no doubt about that. "Please. I want more."

"Agree to my original offer. Become mine while I work this project. Submission isn't a dirty word, you know. It's a precious gift. One I don't take lightly."

Jennifer squeezed her eyes closed and remembered the way her stomach rolled every time he came near her. There were so many nights she spent thinking of him. Imagining what he'd look like without clothes, all the many things he'd force her to do... Her pulse beat between her legs. He simply made her crazy. That's what this had to be.

Liar.

If she couldn't be honest with herself, what chance did she have in the future?

His fingers wriggled, and all the denial fell to the floor. He'd reduced her to a writhing mass of want and need, and she fucking loved it.

"Yes," she whispered, her voice hoarse.

"Say it again." The dark demand grated across something even darker inside her. The one place she dared not go.

"Yes goddamit! I want to be yours. I want to be fucked, used, whatever you want." The admission ripped a hole through the fragile barrier of her mind. The tears she'd desperately held on to burst free, and she sobbed with a wondrous mixture of relief and stark fear.

"Then come for me, love." Her stomach clenched at his words. "Come for the Master you desperately desire."

The last of his words shocked her mind, but it was too late to stop her body's reaction. Through tears and all, Jennifer thrust her hips back, and Daegan shoved three of his fingers into her clenching pussy.

"Let go of the fear, love. You've held on to it for far too long." His lips touched between her shoulder blades. An almost reverent sensation compared to the rough finger fucking between her legs. The combination proved more than she could bear. She thrashed against the bench and tightened her hold on the bars. His fingers slammed into her one last time, igniting the explosion she'd been waiting for. She came with fat tears rolling down her face, sweat covering her body, and the sure knowledge he'd broken something inside her.

"Ahh so beautiful. As eager as you are, I think you're going to be a very fast learner."

She barely comprehended the rest of what he said. Little aftershocks of pleasure continued to crash through her. When her body slumped against the soft leather covering, she felt boneless and unable to move. She had no idea what to expect now. Would he fuck her? He certainly deserved some satisfaction after blowing her mind.

Jennifer tried to form the words to ask the questions, and instead a strange and unintelligible language of exhaustion came out of her mouth.

Daegan laughed behind her. "I have no idea what you said, but I think I get the gist." He leaned over her and removed her hands from the restraints. Once he freed Jennifer, Daegan lifted her into his arms and placed a sweet kiss on her nose. "It's been a long day. You need to get some rest. Things are going to change tomorrow, and we both have a lot to look forward to."

She had a fleeting thought to question his meaning, but her body would have none of it. Her eyes had fluttered closed, and the fatigue began to pull her under. Daegan placed her down on something soft. Automatically she curled into the protective ball she preferred for sleep, and he chuckled some more.

The cushion she lay on shifted, and she realized Daegan had joined her.

"Come here." He twisted her to face him and draped her upper body over his chest. The soft fabric of the shirt he still wore brushed her cheek. She snuggled closer—settling—and immediately heard his heartbeat under her ear.

Thump. Thump. Thump.

She marveled at the sound. Never in her life had she slept with a man. In fact she couldn't remember ever a time when she didn't spend her nights sleeping alone. She should have felt awkward, but the amazing release he'd given her left her too out of it to worry all that much. Plus he smelled nice. There was a faint pine smell underlying his male musk. She inhaled deeply. And maybe just a hint of sweat. He worked hard every day. He might be the architect and contractor for this building, but he definitely had no aversion to getting his hands dirty from hard work.

She'd witnessed that firsthand.

Daegan kissed the top of her head and then began

stroking her hair. Jennifer's eyes rolled back in her head at the ecstasy of such a simple touch. She could get used to this kind of treatment...

You'd better not.

CHAPTER 4

"Well, what in the hell do we have here?"

Jennifer heard the question in some vague part of her brain. At first she thought it was part of the incredible dream she'd been having about her and the devil in the Dark Room. Her pussy was on fire, and she needed some relief. She ground down against the edge of her bed, hoping to find the sweet spot to get her off.

"Wake up, love. We've been caught." Daegan nudged her shoulder.

Unclear whether the voices in her head were real or not, she mumbled, "What?" Her breasts tingled, and her nipples tightened. She didn't want to wake up from a dream that felt this damned good.

Male laughter erupted. "What in the world did you do to her last night? Or do I even want to know?"

The questions jerked Jennifer from her stupor. Her head still floated somewhere above the ground, but enough of reality seeped through for her to realize this wasn't a dream. She'd gone to the Dark Room to find her keys and ended up...

Her memory of the night before came crashing down. She'd submitted to Daegan in more ways than she thought possible. And...and. Oh God, she'd agreed to so much more. The truth compressed her chest, restricting her ability to breathe. Jennifer pressed her hands to the bed with the intent of getting away as fast as she could. Immediately her muscles screamed from overuse, and she collapsed against Daegan's chest. A hard-muscled, well-sculpted one at that with amazingly warm skin that felt like smooth silk under her hand. At some point he'd removed...

Jennifer's eyes widened, and the shock of bright light made her squint. She jerked her head to the right and heaved a sigh of relief to find Daegan still wore pants. That thought was immediately followed by regret. This wasn't part of her life plan.

Is it really such a bad thing to be lying on top of him, both naked and warm? Not to mention aroused?

The familiar heat between her legs sizzled across nerve

endings, and it took everything she had not to moan out loud. She had a nice warm bed at home with a very happy routine that kept her head in the game and not in the clouds of stupid make-believe.

Jennifer crinkled her forehead as more of the night before rushed into her mind. Her Irish devil had given her an explosive orgasm and then simply put her to sleep. He'd not fucked her or even demanded she suck him off. For the first time in a very long time, she'd slept like the dead with not a care in the world. Jennifer shook her head. She really didn't get him or this crazy situation.

Once again, she pushed up on her arms, this time ignoring the aches and pains of the day before. Right now she needed a little ibuprofen and her morning yoga routine to get her feeling normal again. And maybe something to make her forget the colossal mistake of the night before. *Yeah right.* As if any pill could make her forget. Another flash of the pleasure she'd received at Daegan's hands shot through her brain. Did she really want to forget that?

Never.

Lost in her thoughts, she'd failed to notice both men turn silent. When she slowly swiveled her head, she found them both smiling at her like men with a big-ass secret.

"What?"

"I think you've been giving Chase here a show."

Chase laughed. "It wouldn't be the first time."

Something dark and ugly crossed Daegan's face for a brief second before he smoothed out his features and lifted her from his lap. In a split second, he'd maneuvered her behind him, blocking most of her body with his.

"We got locked in last night. Which ended up a stroke of luck as far as I'm concerned."

Jennifer rolled her eyes and crossed her arms across her breasts. In her line of work she had absolutely no issue with her nudity in front of others. Hell, Chase and Murphy had seen her naked more than any other men in her life. Now that her ordeal had ended, she was more than ready to go home. She had a shoot later this afternoon, and she needed a shower desperately. Jennifer slid along the leather and attempted to scoot past Daegan.

He grabbed her wrist and stilled her movements.

"I need to find my clothes so I can get dressed and go home. I've got a schedule to keep."

"Not yet. First we need to talk."

She sighed. This was exactly the kind of discussion she'd been trying to avoid.

"I think that's my cue to leave. Jennifer, I'll see you later." Chase winked at her before disappearing out the door.

"Look, Daegan." She reluctantly turned to face him. "A lot happened last night, and I don't disagree that we should probably discuss it, but I have a shoot this afternoon, and it takes time to prepare." Not that she really wanted to get into all the nitty-gritty details about that.

"Running again?"

She narrowed her eyes and pressed her hands to her hips. "No, I am not running again. I fully remember what happened here last night. As crazy as I think it is for us to take one night and try to turn it into something I don't understand, I'm not going to pretend I didn't mean what I said."

He shifted his stance and stepped closer. "I think crazy is underrated."

Damn. Just when she thought his arrogance would fuel her anger, he turned on her with something different.

Jennifer took a shaky breath. "Why do you do that?"

He smiled. "Do what?"

"Say things that throw me off-balance."

Daegan stared at her for a long moment. "That's nothing compared to this."

"What?" she whispered.

Instead of responding, he cupped his hand behind her neck and pulled her forward until their lips hovered precariously close. Her sudden intake of breath disappeared when their mouths met. His left hand touched her cheek, shattering her almost nonexistent resistance as the kiss turned hot and hard instantly.

Their tongues met and tangled as the sheer strength of his possession consumed her. Unable to catch her breath, she clung to him like a life preserver in a violent storm. Daegan growled into the kiss seconds before his teeth grasped her lower lip and nipped the sensitive skin.

All the reasons she couldn't agree to Daegan's deal evaporated under the incredible onslaught of tongue and teeth working their way around her mouth. The only thing that mattered was the way he made her feel in that moment. Wanted. Cherished. Desired. He made it so easy to let everything else slide away.

Under her hands, his muscles flexed and bunched as she inched her way across the heated flesh of his broad shoulders. Jennifer gave in to her desires and poured everything she'd held back in that kiss. He inspired her to be something she rarely was—honest about her needs.

Pressure built deep in her chest, starting a vibration inside her that escaped from her mouth in a low moan of sweet ecstasy. The fear she'd been swamped with from the moment she'd woken up with troubling memories faded to a distant part of her mind. Not forgotten but demoted to unimportant.

Heat surged between her thighs, preparing for Daegan to take what he so obviously wanted from her. Excitement bubbled in her stomach. She moved her hands, first across his pecs and then trailed her fingers along the faint line of hair that led lower. His abdominal muscles twitched, and his fingers pressed harder to her cheeks, spurring her to keep going until she reached the barrier of his pants. When she tried to attack the button that would remove them, he covered her hands with his and pulled from the kiss.

"Daegan?" She kept her voice low, not wanting to break the moment.

A harsh curse word sounded between them, and Jennifer closed her eyes against it. Tears sprang to her eyes, which she valiantly kept from falling. There was so much tension between them now it felt like hot, thick air on the worst Southern summer day. Daegan rubbed the back of his neck, more evidence of his agitation.

"You need to go now, Jennifer."

She blinked, taken aback by the sudden change in his demeanor. "What?" She definitely didn't understand him at all. The bulge in his pants and the way he touched her indicated that he wanted her, yet he didn't take what he needed. Wasn't that what it was all about? "I don't understand."

"I know you don't. That's why you need to leave now." He backed away from her and scooped her clothes from the floor. "Get dressed."

Jennifer snatched the garments from his hand and hastily put them on. She had no idea what his problem was. He'd asked for her to be honest and that's what she'd tried to do. This attitude of his was for the birds. She'd left her purse in the office before she'd entered the Dark Room last night, but she still needed to find her keys. She turned in the direction of the platform and wanted to cry when she spied the bench he'd had her on last night. Had it only been a few hours ago? It felt like an eternity since he'd had her naked and needy enough to make her agree to his wild offer just to achieve release.

She balled her fist and stuck it in her mouth, biting down until the need to weep passed. Tears brought on by emotions were the weakest kind. She straightened her spine and rounded the seating area on the hunt for her car keys.

"Looking for these?"

She whirled back to him to find her keys dangling from his fingers. Suspicion immediately filled her mind. How did he have those? She started to ask the question and clamped her lips into a thin line.

Get out. Don't engage him anymore.

Sanity stopped her from giving him another chance to make a fool of her. One of these days she'd remember to use her brain first. Determined to save a scrap of self-respect, she stalked toward him only close enough to take the offered prize. If he noticed her movements were jerky and filled with anger, he didn't show a single outward sign. As far as she could tell, he'd turned cold as ice.

She turned to leave, and his hand clamped around her fingers, rendering her immobile.

"I'll meet you here after your shoot. We can go to dinner and discuss how this arrangement between us is going to work."

Jennifer made the mistake of meeting his gaze. For a moment he'd let his guard down and she saw everything. Desire, mirth, and sadness. The last took her aback. Of all the emotions storming through her, she'd never expected his to be so complex. Now she wanted to know why.

Damned curiosity.

"Yes, Daegan." The words came out of her mouth, she knew they did, but she had no idea why. What exactly was wrong with her?

"No more running, little rabbit."

With that, he turned and strode out of the Dark Room, leaving her there in a complete mass of confusion. After a few minutes of standing still at a complete loss, she glanced down at the keys in her hand and remembered she had somewhere to be. With no small amount of effort, she put one foot in front of the other and followed the path blazed by the devil.

She had no idea what time it was, but there was no doubt her schedule was shot. She needed to shove this weird sensation to the back of her mind and concentrate on what needed to be done. When in doubt she could always rely on the comfort of her routine.

And as far as Daegan was concerned... Well, if he wanted to sport blue balls by the end of the day, it was certainly his right. Who was she to tell him what an idiot he was? For a fleeting moment, she'd thought maybe Daegan would be different. She almost laughed out loud.

Jennifer grabbed her purse from Eve's desk and hurried out the door. Whatever tricks he had up his sleeve, she'd handle. She had to.

Daegan stood in his office and looked out the window. Despite the beautiful view of Uptown he had, his gaze remain transfixed on the parking lot below him. Jennifer's dark blue classic '69 Fastback Mustang taunted him—almost as much as the woman did. She'd been in the building for hours, and he'd not seen or heard a word from her. He bided his time, giving her some space to not only think about the night before but also finish her work.

Staring down at the blacktop reminded him of the first time he'd laid eyes on her. She'd pulled into the parking lot on his first day on the job site. At first, it was the classic car purring like a kitten that caught his attention... Until he'd glimpsed a flash of blonde hair as she rounded a curve. He had a hard-on for classic cars, and one with a pretty girl could only be better.

She'd parked in a parking space not far from the door and quickly emerged from the fine machine one incredible bare leg after another. He'd literally held his breath as she stretched to her full height. With a miniskirt that barely covered her ass, she'd been all legs. Whatever Chase had been telling him about the building went in one ear and out the other.

All too quickly, she'd disappeared inside, and he'd been forced to return his focus to the job at hand. Truth be told, the instant attraction bothered him. He wasn't exactly immune to a beautiful woman, but he'd sought her out more than once over the next few weeks. He'd discovered pretty quickly that her beauty came with a hard outer shell she didn't want cracked. She avoided close contact with anyone, which made no sense for a woman whose job it was to get naked, tied up, and photographed in every imaginable scenario.

But there were rare moments when she thought no one was looking, like the night before in the gallery, when the vulnerability he spotted on her face ripped through his resolve.

That was the woman he needed.

Since then, his wanting for the woman was driving him insane. Every instinct he possessed pushed him to claim her. A thought that nearly made him laugh out loud. Jennifer was not that easy. He doubted she'd every truly submitted in her life. At least not in the way he had in mind for her. Daegan shook his head and asked himself why. Why her and why now? The thought of his wife always pushing for more crowded his mind. His commitment to her had led them both astray to almost the very end. One thing had become abundantly clear. He did not need another long-term relationship. Not now. Not ever.

None of which stopped him from his relentless pursuit of Jennifer. He'd approached her numerous times before finally making his latest offer. He needed a short-term arrangement to work whatever this was out of his system, and she needed to be taught how to embrace what her mind and body begged for. Like him, she had desires that could only be ignored for so long. He craved the power dynamic between a submissive and a Dominant. It was impossible to deny the exhilaration he experienced every time he discovered the key to a submissive's pleasure. That's what he sought with Jennifer.

He thought of her eyes. They were often a deep blue with the harsh light of the studio shining down on her. She'd play for the camera, move seductively through pose after pose, but when Chase didn't have the camera pointed in her direction, a wisp of vulnerability would drift across her face. She was bloody good at her job, but something made her sad. After Murphy had nearly spilled the beans about Jennifer's background, Daegan's curiosity had gotten the better of him. He'd pulled some strings and managed to get some basic information about her. Where she lived, how much money she made, that kind of detail. What surprised him more than anything was the sealed file he couldn't get his hands on with any amount of influence. Something had happened when she was a minor that had given the American courts cause to legally emancipate her from her parents at the tender age of sixteen. When most girls were worrying about boyfriends and school, she'd become a legal adult and learned to support herself by taking on the responsibilities that should have been her parents'. According to his information, she'd been alone ever since.

Many sleepless nights since had his mind wandering down too many paths of possibilities. Like today, he'd pulled out the file and combed through it once again. He'd damn near memorized every word, and still he searched. Hoping for a clue that would miraculously tell him everything. Or lay to rest the turmoil she stirred in him.

A twinge of guilt surged through his gut. He didn't imagine Jennifer would enjoy knowing he'd pried into her private life without her knowledge. Hell, even Chase or Murphy would have his ass if they found out. They might be committed to Eve, but they protected Jennifer like a couple of papa bears.

As if on cue, a knock sounded at Daegan's door. He turned away from the window and his wayward thoughts and took a seat behind his desk. "Come in."

Chase entered, looking tired as hell. He had no idea what it took to create the magic his friend did with a camera, but he imagined it wasn't easy. Daegan watched him drop into the leather seat across from his desk and waited patiently for him to talk.

"Long day," Chase said.

"Was it? I know it's been pretty hectic on the construction front. On the upside though, your penthouse condo is going to be finished by next month."

Chase perked up. "Yeah? That's great. As much as we love Eve's apartment, we need more space. But I didn't come by to talk about the building."

Daegan's stomach sank. He wanted to hear his friend out on whatever bothered him, but the clock was ticking on Jennifer. If she got out of the building before he got to her, she'd disappear for the night. Although right now he had no clue how to extricate himself from a long conversation with the man, who, for all intents and purposes, was his boss.

"What's up?" He really didn't like the look on Chase's face. They'd known each other too long for him not to recognize when his friend had something unpleasant to say. "Whatever it is, just spit it out. I can already tell I'm not going to like it."

"What happened last night with you and Jennifer? She's a pro at her job, but the camera picks up on the slightest nuance, and she was off her game today. That shoot took twice as long as it should have."

Immediately Daegan thought of her. If she'd been bound for this job when she'd already been physically taxed the night before...

"Is she all right?"

Chase narrowed his eyes. "Yeah, she's fine. But she's exhausted and needs some rest. But you didn't answer my question."

"And I don't intend to. I think whatever happens between Jennifer and I in our personal lives is private business."

"Look we've been friends a long time—"

"Exactly. So you know I won't hurt her."

Chase heaved a sigh and leaned back in his chair. "You don't know her very well, and I'm afraid she isn't ready for a man like you."

Daegan drew his brows together. "A man like me? I'm like you, so what the hell is that supposed to mean?" Daegan swore under his breath. If Chase had been any other man butting in to his business, he'd be showing him the door. But a decades-long friendship wasn't easy to ignore.

"I don't want her hurt. She looks and acts tough as nails, but she's fragile. Not that you'll ever get her to admit that."

Daegan nodded. "What happened to make her like that?"

Chase shook his head. "Not my story to tell, and you know it. There are some facts that have to be given willingly, and what hurt she carries inside is only for the right man to discover."

"I never knew you to be so romantic."

"Don't fuck with this, Daegan, if you aren't serious. She'll play, don't get me wrong. She's too deep into this world not to need a certain amount of attention. But if you push her for more, you'd better be prepared for the consequences."

Daegan fought to hold his tongue. Yes, Chase was his friend, but he and Murphy were also all the protection Jennifer had, and he suspected she needed it.

"You're a good man, Daegan, but you came here to escape your grief. Eventually, you'll be pulled back to your real life, and I don't think she should get attached. There are a lot of subs at the club that would kill to be your temporary submissive. In fact, I can refer you to many I guarantee you'll enjoy. Don't make Jennifer your rebound woman."

Chase's last words irked the hell out of him. "You make her sound like a sad woman not strong enough to make her own decisions. I like Jennifer, and I have faith in her strength."

His friend nodded. "She is strong, and she'd make an exceptional submissive." Chase pushed his fingers through his hair. "But I'm afraid of what it's going to take to get to that point."

His odd choice of words drove home much of what Daegan already suspected. There were massive walls that had to be broken through. The man who succeeded would be rewarded with a great gift. If he failed...

"I understand," Daegan said calmly.

Chase's expression softened. "You really want this, don't you?"

"Aye, that I do." He answered without a second thought. Along the way he'd find a way to give them both what they needed.

His friend stared long and hard at him. Searching for something when he finally relented. "Then she's waiting for you down in my office,"

CHAPTER 5

*J*ennifer tapped her foot on the floor and screwed her hands tighter together. This waiting here with nothing to do was going to kill her. Fatigue weighed on her almost as much as worry. She'd not been at her best today, and Chase knew it. She suspected that was the reason she sat waiting for him in his office. He was going to want an explanation, and she wasn't about to get into her feelings or lack thereof in regard to his friend Daegan.

Daegan...

He really was the devil. He'd led her into temptation, and now she thought of little else. In one night he'd opened a door she had no idea how to close. Last night in the dark, he'd proven his point with total clarity. Not only did she want him, she also wanted to submit to him. Jennifer trembled from a tingle that traveled the length of her spine at the memory. When she closed her eyes and returned to the scene of her disaster, she felt the burning need across her flesh burning hotter than the night before.

The sound of Daegan's voice at her ear melted her insides, making it so easy to let her guard down. God, she loved his accent. And when he called her love...

"Ready to go, are you?"

"Mmhmm," she murmured. In her head, she'd go anywhere he asked her to. He made her breasts tingle and her pussy moisten with so much anticipation. All day long she'd remembered the delicious pain he'd delivered across her backside when he spanked her. When she'd examined her ass in the mirror this morning, she'd been almost disappointed to see no telltale sign of their night together.

Jennifer blew out a hard breath. What the hell was wrong with her? Why did she crave him of all people to mark her?

"Jennifer. Are you listening to me?"

The shock of his raised voice made Jennifer jump in her seat. Her eyes popped open, and she found Daegan standing over her.

"Wha—" She sat up straight. "What did you say?" Her pulse pounded, blood roared in her ears. She gripped the arm of the chair, and for a split second she considered running from the room.

No more running, rabbit. She heard his words from last night in her head. There was no escape.

"I asked you if you're ready to go."

"Go where? Chase asked me to meet him here."

Daegan brushed her cheek and practically stared right through her. "Chase sent me down here. I guess I'm not the only one who thought you might run tonight."

Jennifer bristled at his answer. It was one thing for her to realize that he'd known more about her than he should and a whole other ball game for him and Chase to start assuming what she needed to do. She'd learned a hell of a long time ago to stand up for herself.

"Where and how I go is my business. It has been since I was sixteen."

"Not tonight, love." Daegan swept her into his arms and wrapped his arm around her waist. "Tonight you need to relax and recharge. I've made it me personal mission."

She eyed him warily. What did he have up his sleeve? She couldn't exactly think straight this close to him. His masculine scent filled her senses and flooded her mind with images from the night before. Somehow being in the Dark Room had made her feel less—on display. It had given her a sense of anonymity that made everything so much easier. That feeling was gone.

Her stomach growled. Mortified, Jennifer hid her face in Daegan's shirt.

"You need to eat, and I know the perfect place."

Too tired to argue anymore, Jennifer allowed Daegan to pull her from Chase's office and out the front door of the building. Sunset had long passed, and Jennifer lifted her gaze to the sky, hoping for a glimpse of a star-filled night. A cool breeze floated across her warmed skin, providing little relief from the war that raged inside her.

"I'm not dressed for dinner," she protested.

"You're fine for what I have in mind." He ushered her to his car and helped her in on the passenger side before returning to the driver's side and sliding behind the wheel. After a few seconds, Jennifer sank into the pale leather seats of Daegan's vintage Mercedes. She'd admired his car from afar, but this was the first time she'd seen it firsthand.

"Nice car."

"From one connoisseur to another. Your Mustang purrs like a kitten."

She couldn't help but smile. She'd had no idea he

noticed. "My mom's second husband owned one, and I loved it. When I was a kid I swore I'd drive one too. I saved for years for that car, but it was worth every penny."

Daegan curled his hand around hers and rubbed his fingers across her knuckles. Her stomach tumbled at the gesture. With a newly formed lump in her throat, she didn't know what else to say. Fortunately, Daegan must have sensed her discomfort, and they drove the rest of the way in silence. Jennifer took a deep breath and relaxed. She enjoyed the quiet. It was a relief to realize he didn't expect her to entertain him every second they were together. Instead she reveled in the intimacy of her hand in his and the simple way he'd managed to put her at ease.

For a few minutes she could pretend this was a date. Her first real date. Not that she'd ever admit that little nugget of humiliating information.

The car slowed, and Jennifer studied their surroundings. He'd driven them to the east side of town not far from the arts district. He pulled into a partially empty lot and eased them into a parking spot. She immediately recognized the Black Finn. An Irish American restaurant she'd passed by often.

"Don't worry. Everything's going to be fine," he assured her. She met his gaze and smiled, thankful for his words.

Before she could respond, he leaned across the seat and kissed her. Warm lips nibbled her mouth with a gentle touch until he coaxed her to open. His tongue touched against hers briefly before he drew away and stepped out of the car.

He led her inside with a flutter of butterflies in her stomach. She'd never experienced this no-nonsense, follow-my-lead side of Daegan. Most of their encounters were either sarcastic and flirty or him aggressively working to get a response out of her. Tonight he seemed almost reverent.

Daegan spoke briefly to the hostess before she led them to the back of the restaurant to an alcove tucked behind a wood-burning fireplace. Jennifer was relieved to discover no other diners at the surrounding tables. Here, amid the candle glow and soft music playing in the background, they could enjoy a nice dinner nearly alone.

A waiter appeared, and Daegan gave their drink and dinner orders. Slightly annoyed by his assumptions, she cleared her throat to catch his attention.

He smiled. "Trust me. I've ordered a sampler of their best selections. All the food is fantastic here." The waiter slipped away quietly, leaving them alone.

"I can't eat stuff like that," she whispered. "I have a shoot tomorrow."

"You can and you will," he replied in that tone that said you will listen and follow.

She wanted to insist. Hell, she felt like standing up and stomping her feet, he made her so mad. Instead, she picked up her glass and took a swallow to keep from blurting out the vicious words about where he could stick his heavy-handed attitude.

"So what happened today?"

Jennifer choked on the water she'd been sipping. "You don't mince words, do you?"

He shrugged. "Life is too short not to get to the point." Daegan intertwined their fingers. She didn't know what to think of his habit of touching her every chance he got. She wasn't accustomed to it.

"I was a little off my game today at work is all. It's not a big deal. Lack of sleep will do that, you know." She hated the defensive tone of her voice, but she couldn't help it. Daegan had a way of getting under her skin no matter what he said or did.

"Then we'll have to take care of that tonight, won't we?" He lifted her hand to his lips and placed a kiss across her knuckles.

She tried to jerk her hand free, and Daegan only tightened his grip. "Don't," he warned.

"I don't know how to do this." she whispered. "I know I

agreed, but this is way..." She didn't want to admit the rest.

"Outside your comfort zone," he finished.

Jennifer nodded. "I think this is a mistake. There are other women, eager women, who'd be more than happy to fill this role for you."

"That's where you're wrong. This isn't just some role that needs to be filled. It's not a game. In fact, when I came here, I had no intention of getting involved with anyone. But if there's one lesson in life I have learned more clearly than I like, it's that life rarely goes exactly as you planned. Real life is messy."

Didn't she know it? She'd been living that messy life for as long as she could remember. Not that she wanted to wallow there. Those days were behind her. "I know. It's just..."

"You're afraid."

Jennifer reared back as if she'd been slapped. Every time he managed to say something that hit a nerve, she wanted to flee.

"Wait. Hear me out." He rubbed his thumb across her knuckles and soothed her ruffled feathers just like that. "You want something you don't understand, so you push it away. It's a natural reaction. You head is in one place, and your body is in another."

God, he was right. She was acting like a child. An all-too-familiar bitterness from her past reared its ugly head. She didn't belong here any more than she'd belonged there. Sadness ached inside her. How would she ever overcome the past completely if she didn't learn to at least trust one person? Chase and Murphy were both honest with her, and she'd shared a little, but even Eve, who'd tried so hard to befriend her the last six months hadn't gotten very far.

"I'm not sure what I want anymore. I'm confused," she blurted before she could bite back the words.

The surprise on Daegan's face melted into a slow smile. "Why do I get the feeling that's the most honest thing you've said so far?"

Jennifer didn't respond. Once again she found herself at a loss for words.

"Sometimes what a submissive wants is different from what she needs. It's my job as a Dom to figure out the difference in each situation." He placed a quick kiss on the tips of her fingers. "Sometimes she needs a comforting touch, or pleasure beyond her wildest dreams." His tongue flicked across her flesh. "But sometimes she needs her Dom to make the hard decisions such as deciding when her limits should be pushed or doling out any punishment she has earned. All of those details will be up to me to decide."

Jennifer opened her mouth and gasped for breath. Her whole body tightened and grew hot.

"Punishment?"

"Yes, love. What punishment you receive will depend on what rules you break. Some are more severe than others."

Rules? Was he kidding? The only rules she lived by were of her own making and there were few. Always be professional. No one but she could drive her car. And never ever let anyone get too close.

Daegan kissed her hand and laid it back on the table. "Don't worry about that yet. We'll get to that when we get back home. For now, let's relax and enjoy dinner. You need to get as much rest as possible tonight."

She swallowed thickly, still stunned by his comments on punishment. She wanted to know more but was afraid to ask. Growing up in between two families she didn't exactly belong to had left her an outcast. She'd seen her father take a belt to her half brother and sister several times when they'd misbehaved, but he'd never done the same to her. And when she'd been with her mother's family, they'd barely acknowledged her, let alone ever punished her.

For many years, she'd wondered why she'd been treated differently until she'd asked a friend who'd easily supplied the answer with a shrug. *"It's what families do. Parents are expected to punish and reward their kids appropriately."*

The statement had stunned her. *Families.* They took care of their own and kids like her were left alone. Always alone...

In an incredible bout of timing, their dinner arrived and the conversation changed. Daegan talked animatedly about the building progress on the Pleasure Playground, and she picked at her food, eating only enough to keep him from commenting on her lack of appetite.

The exhaustion of her day returned in full force, and it took everything she had not to fall face-first into her plate of food. With childhood memories threatening to drag her down, her thoughts turned to escape. That thought made her go stock-still. Maybe Daegan was right. She did have a habit of running away from situations that made her the slightest bit uncomfortable.

What the hell? If she got up and walked out now, what would she gain? She'd be walking away from a gorgeous, intelligent man with a wicked streak that intrigued her. For what? An empty apartment? More nights at the club that gave her just enough to get by? Was that all she wanted for her life? To get by?

Desolation pulled on Jennifer's resolve. If she wasn't careful, she'd slide into a deep depression and be back at square one all over again. Blinking back tears, she straightened her spine and focused on what Daegan had to say. She'd fought back at the age of sixteen and after more than a decade of getting by, she was going to take a risk.

"Jennifer, are you listening?"

When she finally snapped out of it, she found Daegan staring at her with concern. A hot flush spread across her skin. His shrewd gaze followed the line of heat. The way he looked at her always made her think he saw clear through to her soul. As if he, and he alone, saw her truths. She found it unsettling...and arousing.

"I think we should get you home now." He hastily signed the bill she'd not even noticed be delivered and pulled her from the booth without waiting for a response.

Grateful for his take-charge demeanor, she followed his lead. She took his firm grasp of her hand as a further sign of his strength. Something she sorely needed at the moment. Her brain started to turn those thoughts over, and she forced it to stop. She was sick to death of analyzing every desire that entered her mind. So what if she wanted a man to take care of her sometimes. Was it really too much to hope for?

WHEN THEY ARRIVED BACK at the Playground,

Jennifer stared wistfully at her car. She was still torn between the familiar and the unknown. Luckily for her, Daegan didn't miss her reaction, and he squeezed her knee in a comforting gesture.

"You'll stay with me."

It was a statement, not a question, and luckily for them both she didn't have the energy to argue. He led her inside and into a section where she'd never ventured. This hall had yet to be touched with construction and from the outside, it didn't look like much. "Your apartment is down here?"

Daegan smiled and nodded. "Don't worry. I'm not planning to keep you in a dump. A few of the new condos should be done within a couple of weeks, but those are earmarked for specific buyers already. So I took some liberties and upgraded this old place for me self. I'm going to be here for a while, so I thought I might as well make it comfortable."

He opened the door, and she looked around in shock. Comfortable didn't begin to describe what she saw. The living room was very small by most people's standards, but he'd filled it with dark, comfortable furniture, hardwood floors, large throw rugs and a lot of plants. The greenery in the space really shocked her.

"Do you have a green thumb or something?" She marveled at the trees and potted plants that dotted every surface. When Daegan didn't answer right away, she turned back to him and caught the flicker of unease across his face.

"It reminds me of home."

"Ireland, you mean?" She wandered over to an enormous pot of sweet potato vine and wondered how the heck he got it to grow like that indoors.

"Yes."

"If you love it so much, why did you leave?"

"I needed a change."

His abrupt answers left her with more questions than answers, but tonight wasn't the night to push. She'd sensed a change in him the moment they walked into his domain. A current of tension filled the room.

"Take off your clothes, Jennifer," Daegan demanded.

She whirled on him to find his dark gaze boring down on her. The smart-ass response she'd been prepared to fling his way died on her tongue.

"You should know that I expect obedience from a submissive. You'll not be using me like the men at the club. If I ask you a question, I'll expect your honest answer. If there is something you don't like you can tell me, but it will be up to me to decide if you need it or not. Is that understood?"

Instinct made Jennifer want to fight against what he said. But deep down he'd accessed a part of her so intrinsic to who she was, that she knew not to fight him on this. She didn't want to. "Yes, Sir."

"Good. But, Jennifer." He hesitated. "You aren't removing your clothes yet."

With trembling hands, she began to remove her blouse. With each button, the tension grew. This nervousness didn't make sense to her. How many times had Daegan already seen her without clothes? He'd attended every one of her demonstrations since they'd met months ago. She eased the blouse from her shoulders, and Daegan held out his hand for the garment. She repeated the process with her small skirt and shoes until she stood in front of him in a tiny thong and matching plum-colored bra.

"That color suits you. The creamy color of your skin against the dark, rich color." The husky tone of his voice sent a shiver racing along her spine. One minute she felt confused, and the next ready to melt at his feet.

He stepped into her personal space and brushed a finger along her collarbone before slipping underneath her bra strap. She shivered under his touch. Daegan had a way of turning every inch of her body into an erogenous zone with a simple touch.

"You play at the club a lot. Do you have sex with them?"

"Rarely," she whispered.

"When was the last time?" He pulled the strap from her arm.

"I-I'm not sure. Maybe a few months or more." Her head buzzed from his attention.

"And protection?" His hand caressed the underside of her bared breast.

"Always. Birth control shots and condoms. And Chase requires I get tested every month because of the work we do." She struggled for air. His finger had begun tracing circles around her areola.

"Do you want me to fuck you, Jennifer?"

Her eyes widened. "Why do you keep asking me all these questions? I thought you wanted me to get some rest."

His fingers pinched her nipple in a vise-tight grip. Pain exploded across her senses. "A question is not an answer. I hadn't planned on punishment tonight, but I won't hesitate if you persist."

Warmth flooded Jennifer's sex despite the unbelievable pain he administered to her nipple. She imagined him bending her over his knee and spanking her again. Her stomach trembled.

"Now answer the question."

Her sex squeezed. "Yes, I want you to fuck me." It made her a little crazy to admit it. Like saying it could make it happen.

"Was that really that difficult?"

She lowered her eyes. He had no idea.

Daegan sighed. "Take off the rest of your clothes and get up on the bed, in the middle and on your back." He disappeared into another room, and Jennifer moved to follow his commands. She entered the sparsely furnished small bedroom. Where the living room had been decorated and made as comfortable as possible, it seemed this room held little importance in comparison. Other than the queen-size bed and a small wooden dresser against the wall, there was no other furniture.

She spied a stack of books on the floor next to the bed, but in her haste to follow Daegan's request, she opted not to check them out. There would probably be more time later for her to get to know the man behind the Dom.

With her undergarments removed and placed on top of the dresser, she scrambled in place in the middle of his mattress. The cool silk sheets felt heavenly against the hot flush of her skin. She didn't know where to place her arms and legs so she chose to fold her arms across her waist, close her eyes and wait.

"Good girl." Daegan's breath brushed across her shoulder, very close to her ear. "Now spread your legs wide for me."

She complied, a fresh wave of warmth pooling between her thighs. Daegan lifted her foot, and she immediately recognized the sensation of soft leather being wrapped around her ankle.

"I'm going to restrain you, and then once I have your full attention, we'll talk some more."

Jennifer whimpered. It wasn't talk her body ached for at this point. Like her scenes at the club, the cuffs restraining her legs and now her arms worked as a trigger of anticipation for the sweet pain that would soon follow. She craved it to the point her stomach clenched and her heart beat wildly.

"Look at me, Jennifer. I want to see your eyes. They are the windows to your truth."

Jennifer turned her head and met his blazing blue gaze. The stern expression on his face made her shake, not in fear, no; something entirely different.

"It's time to set some rules, Jennifer love."

A small tip of leather touched her inner thigh,

reminding her of... She raised her head and saw that yes, Daegan did indeed have a crop in his hand. The long black implement extended from his hand like it belonged there. She sucked in air and exhaled nice and slow. She needed to calm her racing pulse. Unfortunately nothing stopped the subtle shake of her legs as he trailed the leather strip along her flesh to her ankle.

"Are you listening?"

She met his gaze. "Yes, Sir." Normally she had to force herself to use the expected term of respect at the club during play, but with Daegan it seemed to roll off her tongue almost naturally.

"Good girl." He switched legs. "I'm very excited that you've agreed to my original offer. But there's something you need to keep in mind. Many things actually. This isn't going to be easy. I can tell you're pretty set in your ways of how you like things done. In both work and play. I have different ideas, however. There will be rules for you to follow. Not many, but they are absolute. And in case you have it in your mind that rules are made to be broken. Trust me these are not."

Daegan began a steady tap of the crop on the inside of her thigh. Not even a slap, but it made damn sure he had her undivided attention. While her outside remained mostly still, her insides shook uncontrollably. He was going to kill her with anticipation.

"Rule number one. You will live here with me for the duration of our contract."

Thwap.

A sharp sting bloomed on the inside of her thigh, shooting a blessed pain across every inch of her burning skin. Jennifer gasped in delight. When the initial shock of the first strike began to fade, she noticed the heat and moisture gathering between her legs. Immediately she craved more.

"Rule number two. There will be no more visits to the club unless it's under my direction."

Air whipped across her flesh a mere second before two successive blows rained down on the inside of her opposite leg. This time she moaned at the immediate mixture of pain and pleasure. Her gaze settled on his full, sensual mouth. Her nipples tightened and tingled as she longed to feel his lips surround them. More heat burned inside her.

Daegan walked to the head of the bed and hooked his thumb in her mouth, drawing her gaze to his. "Are you still listening?"

She nodded as much as his grip would allow.

"Good. Three more rules. Are you ready?"

"Yes." She tried to calculate in her head how many more swats with the crop that would be but gave up the minute he touched that little scrap of leather to her stomach. He teased and twirled it around her navel while she held her breath.

"You are a very beautiful woman, but you are too thin. Even for a model."

"I have to be like this."

"No, you don't. Which brings me to rule number three. No more dieting."

Her eyes flew open in shock a breath before the crop landed along the outside of her leg. She cried out, twisting in her restraints. Hunger for more of Daegan burned inside her despite his outrageous demand. To make matters worse, he'd begun fondling her breast, circling one nipple, then the other until her mind swirled with want and need beyond what she thought she could handle. In the blink of an eye, she forgot why she'd been shocked.

His fingers tightened on one rigid tip, giving it a rough pinch that sent a stab of desire straight to her clit. Nerve endings fired to life, and a throbbing between her legs joined the ache in her breasts. Moan after moan fell from her lips as he continued to work her sensitive peaks. First a pinch of pain, then a rub of pleasure. Repeated over and over.

When he bent to bring his mouth to her breast, she noticed the matching hunger and determination in his eyes. He doled out rules and threatened her with punishment, then drove her completely wild with pleasure. She didn't fully understand why he wanted things this way, but she'd begun to see his points very clearly.

His tongue swirled around the nipple, teasing her to her limits before he suddenly tightened his soft lips around her flesh and sucked—hard.

"Ohhh..." She yanked at her wrist cuffs, desperate to touch him. Pull him closer or push him away, she had no idea.

He gently bit her flesh, the scrape of teeth taking her completely by surprise with the ferocity of the sensations. She was falling, losing control. She'd do anything. Her hips arched from the bed almost of their own volition. Her body begged for more, but soft alarm bells began to ring in the back of her head. She wanted too much. Want led to need and need led to destruction. She stiffened.

Daegan lifted his head and stared at her with caution lacing his features. Once again she had the sense that he saw into her soul and somehow knew. He eased from the bed and returned to his place between her legs. He traced the soft leather tip of his crop across the outer folds of her pussy, grazing her clit. She tried not to react, but her body shivered nonetheless.

"Don't be afraid of the truth, love. Yearning to submit can be as natural as taking a breath. When you don't fight it."

He was right. Her head said no, and her body urged for more with every new touch or word he spoke. She suddenly felt like banging her head on the wall. Instead anxiety rose with no outlet; her mind raced. "I —can't—I mean I don't know...how."

"It's okay to be afraid." He leaned forward, placing his mouth just above her pussy. "Just don't let the fear win, Jennifer." Her name whispered across her skin.

God she was so screwed up. One minute this, and one minute that. How had she become so indecisive? Or worse—fearful.

"I can tell it's difficult for you to trust. But why is that? What happened to make you so skittish of your own needs?"

With one little question her mind turned to panic. No way in hell. She struggled viciously against her bindings. She had to get free.

"Jennifer. Stop."

She saw his frown and tried to ignore it although her body stilled nonetheless. This compulsion to obey confused her.

"You agreed to my offer, did you not? To be my submissive for the duration of my time here?"

She nodded with tears welling in her eyes.

"Fear is no reason to give up. It's fighting that very need to run that will get you where you ultimately want to go. Do you really want to give up on the chance I might be right?"

A broken sob slipped from her lips. She had no idea how to deal with the fever burning inside her. "No," she mumbled.

"No, what?" His frown deepened.

He was really going to make her voice every single word. "No, Sir. I don't want to give up."

He brushed the tears away from her cheeks. "You are braver than you know, love. I'm proud of you." He rose to his feet.

Her stomach tumbled at the sight of the crop he bounced on his hand. "Then we'd better finish going over the rules."

With her heart pounding, she sucked in air as she waited for his next words.

"Rule number four." He teased her slit with the end of his crop, bringing her right back to the edge with a few swipes across her clit. "There will be no modeling during our agreement."

"I will no—" Her mind burned for half a second before the crop landed on her leg, stealing her breath. At the same time his finger prodded at her opening. She sucked in air, her stomach muscles tightening. She wanted this so bad.

He slid his finger inside her. The easy glide against slick and swollen tissues felt unbelievable. Then it got really good. Daegan moved his hand in a simple in-and-out motion that drove her wild. She clenched her fists, and her muscles strained against her bindings. She wasn't exactly trying to get loose, but she wanted more.

Her pussy squeezed around him, and someone moaned. She had no idea if the sound had come from her or him. Then his finger slipped free. Before she could protest, he returned with two fingers spreading her open. Wet warmth covered her sex, and she lifted her head to see his dark hair blocking her view as he ate at her pussy. His tongue stroked over her, up one side and down the other before circling the biggest bundle of nerves.

Spine-tingling tension grew in a spot at her lower back. She held her breath as the explosion neared. She barely moved, afraid to jar him from his perfect positioning. Tongue on clit; fingers fucking pussy.

He lifted his head, instantly stopping her race to the ledge. "Nooo," she wailed.

"And that brings us to rule number five."

His fingers stroked inside her twice more before they too disappeared, leaving her empty—adrift. Oh please God, let this mean he was finally going to fuck her. How he'd managed to hold off this long she couldn't imagine. The man had balls of steel or something.

But he didn't remove his pants or climb on top of the bed. He simply picked up the crop, stood straight, and stared down at her with such wicked intent she almost spontaneously combusted.

"Rule number five is simple but very important. Under no circumstances will you have an orgasm until I say you are ready."

CHAPTER 6

*D*aegan watched the understanding bloom on little Jennifer's face. She was a woman who barely expressed any emotion through words, but he could read her like a book. Fear, anger, want, desire... They were all there. He imagined the overload she had to be feeling by now. It had been a long couple of days, and the scene he'd planned for tonight had changed as he'd learned more about her.

The sight of her as she was now nearly undid him. Spread out and open, her pussy glistening and probably aching for him to fuck her. It would be so easy to take her now. Slide into her nice and slow and watch the glorious emotions roll across her face. He shook his head and pushed the image away.

Instead he rounded the bed and rested the crop across her belly. It would serve as a reminder that she was still under his control. He didn't miss the quiver that rippled across her flesh or the puckering of the skin around her nipples. God, she was so damned beautiful. Her responsiveness made him crazy with want for her.

"Why are you doing this?" Her question interrupted his errant thoughts and returned his focus to the task at hand.

He stroked his finger across her collarbone and along the curve of her neck. There was no doubt why Chase used her so extensively in his studio. What he didn't understand is why she never went beyond the superficial. She worked long hours at her job and then occasionally spent time at the club with different Doms who clearly wanted nothing more from her than quick satisfaction. Usually in the form of temporarily marking her exquisite body.

"That's a fair question, love. Unfortunately, you hold the answers, not me. You want this so bad I bet you can practically taste it. Yet you have somehow turned sex and pain into a shield of sorts. You hide behind the physical acts with the hope no one will take the time to look further. That's not me. I want more than that from you. I expect it." Watching Jennifer struggle with the desire to give in versus being uncomfortable with his demands turned him the fuck on.

He leaned forward, and her mouth opened slightly. It was an unconscious invitation on her part, he was certain, but an invitation nonetheless. He took it. Daegan leaned forward and pressed his lips to her mouth, tracing the edges with his tongue. The small gasp she rewarded him with made him press further. He'd pushed her quite a bit, and she had a lot to think about, but first he needed this. He deepened the kiss and ran his bare hands over her nude form. It was his reminder that as long as she remained here with him, he would be in control. Not only would her body be available to him, but also he'd get inside her head every chance he got. Finding out what made her tick and uncovering new ways to push past her fears would become his favorite pastime.

Daegan kneaded the tense muscles of her arms, marveling at the incredible feel of her soft skin. She flexed against her restraints more than once, and he smiled into her mouth with much satisfaction. When she finally began to relax and the coiled tension inside her seemed to ease, he reluctantly pulled from her mouth.

There was a storm brewing. Yes, he could ease the ache between her legs, but then she'd be right back where they started. No. He'd have to sit back and watch what happened next before he took them any further. She had a decision to make. He'd laid out rules he doubted had fully sunk in yet. Now it was time to change her focus.

Of course none of his reasonable thoughts helped the ache of his own body. As much as he wanted to satiate his desires with the beautiful sub in his bed, he needed time to reassess these feelings. It had been a long time since he'd wanted someone this much, and it left him with more than a little unease. No matter how deep he traveled into a submissive's mind for pleasure, when it came to the day-to-day of life he had to have an equal partner. He'd already made one mistake, so he doubted he could afford another.

He unbuckled the restraints at her wrists and rubbed the chafed skin underneath. "I imagine you have some questions," he stated. He didn't expect an answer and purposefully avoided eye contact while he continued to care for her. She needed a few minutes of privacy with her thoughts or she might say something they'd both regret. Satisfied her arms and hands were in good condition, he moved on to her ankles. He removed the bindings from her slim ankles and rubbed the area to ensure good blood flow. Her bright blue painted toes were a contrast he didn't expect from a woman who worked so hard to hide her true self. Much like the fact she'd become a fetish model. For someone who kept her innermost thoughts inside, she certainly enjoyed putting her body on display.

When he let go of her, the first thing she did was scramble under a sheet. He shook his head and lifted his gaze to meet hers.

"Let's hear it," he prompted. It didn't take a genius to see she was stressed.

"You can't really expect me not to work for the next however many months just so you can fuck me. My job isn't about sex. At least not to me." Her voice trembled with anger.

Did she have any idea how much her sassy mouth fired his blood. Right then the urge to curb her coming outburst with his dick in her sassy mouth pressed down on him. He shook it off. *Not yet.*

"I didn't say anything about not working. I said you can't model."

"Same difference. It's a ridiculous demand, and you know it. I have responsibilities. Chase and Murphy count on me. I can't just walk away from that for an experiment. I've worked too hard for this career to give it up now."

Her reference to their potential Dom/sub relationship as an experiment rubbed him wrong. There were so many things he intended to teach her if she got past this. He brushed the annoyance aside. "I've already talked to Chase about this, and he's in complete agreement. He says it's been a long time since you took any kind of break from modeling, and since it's bloody tough on your body, he thinks it's a terrific idea and about time you took a hiatus."

"You did what?" she exploded. He practically saw her vibrating with anger. "How dare you talk to my boss about me behind my back."

"It's what Doms do. We watch and observe and then decide based on what we've seen and heard what is best for you. It's your job to trust in me that I have only your best interests at heart and would never do anything permanently destructive." He gentled his voice. "You aren't losing your job, love. Just getting a temporary reassignment. Give it a chance."

Her eyes narrowed. "What kind of temporary assignment?"

"Eve needs some help with Pleasure Playground. In case you haven't noticed, the poor girl is overworked. Besides trying to manage Altered Ego, the retail shops are set to open over the next six months, which means she has to interview and arrange for the appropriate kind of businesses that fit in with their vision. That's going to take a lot of time."

Jennifer rolled her eyes. "You expect me to work as a secretary? Are you kidding? I've never spent a day of my life behind a desk, and I like computers even less. I've seen her work. She seems more than efficient enough to handle whatever comes up."

Daegan lifted the edge of the sheet and gently tugged the covering from her body. "She's swamped. Chase was planning to hire someone soon anyway. This way Eve gets the help she needs, and you and I get the time we need to test drive the Dom/sub dynamic between us."

"Jesus, Daegan. I'm not a car. A fucking test drive? Seriously?" Jennifer jumped to her feet, putting herself in a position where she towered over him. She stood with fire in her eyes and hands firmly planted on her hips, and he found himself turned on more than ever. He grabbed her wrist and pulled her down to her knees.

"I love your fire. It drives me crazy. It also makes me want to control it." He threaded his hands into her hair and tugged her head back, exposing her neck and throat. Unable to resist, he fastened his mouth to her neck and began to bite down on the tender flesh. Not enough to break the skin but more than enough for her to feel a bite of pain. She moaned. He bit at her skin over and over. Up one side and down the other. His bites would leave marks for several hours.

Mine.

He wanted nothing more than to push her to all fours, mount her, and fuck her.

She wasn't ready.

Once she accepted all of his rules. *Really* accepted them. Then he could take things to the next level.

Until then, he needed to give her some space. He'd roll the dice and take a gamble. All his life he'd enjoyed playing games of chance, and his little hellcat had a choice to make before they went any further.

He wrenched free from her mouth and let go of her hair. Blood surged to his cock at the sight of the red marks he'd left behind. Not to mention the glassy lust shining from her eyes. He could push her to the mattress and take what he wanted. He was certain. "I took the liberty of having dessert delivered, and I suspect it should be here any minute. Go on in the kitchen and have a seat. You can wait for me while I take a quick shower."

Her eyes flared with an emotion he couldn't quite name. Where he'd expected resistance and anger, she'd for a second given him something entirely different. If he hadn't known better, he'd have thought her feelings were hurt. He cupped her face, pulling her close. "When I finish, I'm going to feed you again. Then you'll get down on your knees and tell me you accept my rules." Daegan kissed her quick and hard, reminding her that not only did he want to do this for him, but he wanted it for her. Whatever held her back, she didn't deserve. But he wouldn't force this on her. She would have to take the next step.

Using every ounce of strength he possessed, he walked away. There were other ways to get what he wanted.

Seduction for one. He could have bent her over and fucked her until she said yes—and she would have. Daegan closed the bathroom door behind him and rested his forehead on the opposite side. That wasn't the way he wanted her. His instincts about her ran deep, and he knew for certain coercion would never last long. She'd fight him every step of the way. Of course none of that knowledge did a bloody thing to relieve the ache in his dick or the pressure squeezing his chest.

Looking for some relief, he unzipped his pants and freed his erection. He then fisted his cock and began slow and easy strokes along the aching flesh. Masturbation definitely wasn't what he had in mind, but if he wanted to deal with her with a clear head, then he had to do something. He couldn't stop thinking about the image of her bound and spread on his bed. All that smooth creamy skin practically begged for more than a few swats with his crop. He imagined spending hours with her and a flogger, bringing out a lovely shade of pink from head to toe.

It had been so long since he'd felt a sweet longing such as this. Normally these feelings would have had him running for the hills, given his last few years. He'd moved to the States to escape, and somewhere along the way, he'd begun to heal. After a while he'd begun to realize that while he could live well without a submissive, the lack of one took a lot of pleasure out of his life.

Then he'd met Jennifer in the middle of a photo shoot. She'd been naked except for a pair of thigh-high boots, and he'd been enchanted by the expression on her face as Murphy bound her from breasts to ankles with thick black rope.

Whether she was ready to admit it or not, she used her job for far more than a paycheck. Everything about her changed the minute a scene began. Either at the club or in the studio. From that day on, he'd found ways to observe some of her shoots, and then when he'd discovered her participation at the local BDSM club, he'd watched her there as well. He wasn't surprised she didn't engage in actual penetration all that often. Her needs ran deep. She went to the club for something other than simply getting off.

Daegan tightened his grip and stroked harder. This wasn't going to take long with the wild images of Jennifer running through his mind like a porno film. Before he knew it, his body began to tingle at the base of his spine. The rising orgasm drew closer. He bit back a groan when the first spurt hit the back of the door. Frustration warred with relief as he continued to pump until he was completely spent.

Outside the bathroom, a door slammed closed. Daegan froze. It couldn't be. He quickly re-dressed, cleaned up, and yanked the door open. Silence. That's all he heard. He moved quickly to the kitchen holding his breath until he saw Jennifer on her knees at his table. Only that's not what he found.

Empty. His goddamned apartment was empty.

Daegan glanced around, unwilling to believe the facts right in front of his face. He'd planned to give her space while he took a nice long shower, not drive her to run away. He shoved his hands into his hair and blew out a hard breath. What the hell was he supposed to do now? Daegan dropped into one of the kitchen chairs. "I should have known." He'd gone too far. Not that it made him want to do anything different. He'd put a lot of thought into her rules and had expected her not to take them so easily. Her job and the club had become her identity, and taking those away was meant to make her vulnerable.

That thought made him sit up straight and take notice. Why was getting so deep inside her head so important? He'd decided she would be his first in-depth foray back into the world of D/s since his wife died. That didn't mean he wanted the kind of long-term relationship he'd been steering Jennifer toward without even real-izing it. Hadn't he learned with his wife?

Claire.

Daegan rested his head on his hands and closed his eyes. His relationship with her had evolved slowly for years before he'd decided to put a collar on her, and more years had passed before he'd agreed to take Claire deeper. Her desire to be a 24-7 slave had made him uncomfortable, but by then she'd become his wife and he felt a duty to give her what she needed even if that meant going outside his own boundaries. In the end, his wife had thrived, and he'd grown resentful. Guilt tore through him. She deserved a better memory than that.

So why would he want to push Jennifer so hard now? God, he didn't want to get into this. He was sick to death of the second-guessing and constant analyzing of every move. He still needed a shower, and then he'd dig up some bourbon before he went any further.

Either way, Jennifer had walked out. Common sense told him to let her go, move on. Except with her it wasn't quite that cut-and-dried. Instead, he needed a new plan. They'd start over if they had to. It was high time they both moved on from the ghosts of the past.

Whatever happened tonight or tomorrow, he had a gut feeling this wasn't over.

CHAPTER 7

*J*ennifer stood at her car door, legs trembling and hands shaking. She needed to get in her car and drive far away from here as fast as possible. When Daegan discovered her gone, he was not going to be happy. He'd probably come looking for her, and she couldn't face him now. Unfortunately, her body was being uncooperative. With her key at the ready, she reached for the lock, and her hand shook harder. Tears streamed down her cheeks and into her mouth and none of it mattered.

She'd run. She'd done exactly what he said she would. Her head buzzed with the words he'd spoken the night before. Disappointment slashed deep.

So what. She didn't owe him a thing. She'd agreed to his offer in the heat of the moment before she'd had time to think about it. It wasn't like her to make spur-of-the-moment decisions. Over the years, she'd learned to carefully consider all of her options and not rush into anything with the potential to backfire on her. Jennifer laughed through the tears. What a joke. She was like her mother always said. Fickle.

"One minute you want one thing, and the next it's something else. Which one is it, Jennifer?"

She heard her mother's voice in her head as if it'd been yesterday, not a decade ago. How long had it been since she'd talked to her mother? A sob sounded in her throat. She had to get out of there before someone found her like this. She tried again to put the key in the lock, and the keys slipped from her hand.

"Fuck!"

Jennifer slid to the ground and plopped on her butt. She couldn't drive across town like this. Maybe she could hide in the studio until she got herself under control. Yeah right. The minute Daegan found her car in the parking lot, the first place he'd look was the stupid studio. Thanks to his role as contractor, he had access to the entire building. There was nowhere for her to go. With trembling hands she fished her cell phone out of her purse and turned it on.

Who are you going to call?

She had no one. Story of her fucked-up life. For now her life consisted of her career. Friends were hard to come by, but she kind of had a few. She considered Chase and Murphy her friends, even if they'd betrayed her with that asshole and allowed him to say she couldn't work. Jennifer swiped at the tears that continued to flow. There'd be no talking to them. She'd watched them interact with Eve when they didn't realize she was looking. Her friend submitted to them on a level she couldn't comprehend. No matter what they asked for, she gave willingly. And with a smile on her face. Hell, the woman practically glowed.

Eve. That's it. She jerked open the cell phone and dialed the number she knew by heart before she had a chance to change her mind.

On the fourth ring, Jennifer's hope wilted. Not available. Then Eve answered.

"It's-a-Jennifer," she spat, knowing there was no way to hide her distress.

"What's wrong? Are you all right? You sound like you're crying."

Regret lanced through Jennifer. This was a dumb idea. She began to pull the phone away from her ear and disconnect.

"Don't you dare hang up on me, young lady. Where are

you?" The demand in Eve's voice startled her. She'd never heard the other woman talk like that before.

"Downstairs," she whispered.

"Good, don't move. Seriously, if you don't wait for me, I'll have Murphy track you down and whip your hide. You know he'll do it."

Jennifer nodded her head and felt a ghost of a smile cross her face. "Okay," she mumbled. "I'm in the parking lot." She folded the phone and pushed it into her pocket. She had about two minutes before Eve found her, and she didn't know what to do. There'd be no hiding the tears or getting cleaned up. With one last glance at her car and her only chance for escape, she turned and shuffled back toward the building.

Eve burst through the door, and all the emotion inside Jennifer boiled over. "I tried to run," she blurted.

Her friend wrapped her arms around her. "Of course you did, sweetie."

She held up her shaking hands. "Fingers wouldn't work. Can barely hold the keys." She knew the words tumbling from her mouth made little sense, but they were the best she could do at the moment.

"Come back inside, and you can tell me what happened." Eve ushered her through the front door and steered her in the direction of the studio. "In here."

She pointed to Chase's private office, and Jennifer hesitated.

"Don't worry. Chase and Murphy aren't here."

"But Daegan—"

"Won't dare come in here without an invitation. Trust me."

Trust her. Eve had no idea how foreign those words were to her. And what the hell was up with everyone today pushing her to trust them? Jennifer gritted her teeth against the desire to spit on that word.

"Have a seat. I'll grab us both a drink. I think we're going to need it."

Jennifer nodded before collapsing into the closest chair. Eve reached into the credenza behind Chase's desk and pulled out a bottle of vodka and two tumblers. Desperate to think of anything other than what had happened with Daegan, she sat mesmerized while watching Eve go about retrieving ice, pouring generous shots of the alcohol into the glasses, and restoring things back to their original order. Even in the face of a crisis, the woman had efficiency down to a science.

She swatted at the fresh tears trickling down her face before Eve could see them.

"Here, drink this. It'll help." The other woman thrust a glass into her hand and waited while she gulped at the clear liquid. Instantly the fiery burn singed her throat, and Jennifer began to cough uncontrollably. She grabbed the box of tissues Eve had set out on the coffee table and swiped at her watering eyes and worked to get herself under control. After a few minutes, the burn receded, and she was left with a warm sensation low in her belly. In a not so ladylike fashion, Jennifer blew her nose and lifted her lashes to find Eve waiting patiently across from her.

"Better?"

She nodded.

"Good. Now tell me what happened. Every detail from the beginning. I want to help you."

"Why?"

"Jesus, Jennifer. Why not? We work together all the time. My men care about you a lot, and that means something to me. I'm actually flattered you called me."

"I didn't have anyone else."

Eve winced.

"I mean..."

Her friend held up her hand. "I know what you mean, and I'm still flattered. Leaning on anyone is hard for you."

She wasn't sure that was meant as a question or not.

Either way she had no desire to go down that road. "Daegan wants to dominate me."

Eve laughed. "That's not exactly news, hon. That man's been after you since he laid eyes on you. I take it he finally made a move."

Jennifer felt her eyes widen. "You knew?" Stunned, she waved away a response from Eve. "Doesn't matter, I guess. Last night we ended up locked in the Dark Room together."

"Seriously? Holy crap. I couldn't have planned something that good. And believe me if the two of you didn't do something soon, I was going to do it for you. Do you have any idea how frustrating it has been to watch you two circle each other for months?"

Speechless again, she simply gaped at Eve.

"So I take it things didn't go well in the Dark Room?"

"I couldn't resist him. God, how I've tried. But last night it was too much. His voice in the dark, my—my... Dammit. It's been too long since I've gone to the club, I didn't know what else to do."

Eve leaned forward and placed a hand on her knee. "Stop beating yourself up over this. Face the need, Jennifer. It's what drives you to the club when you can't take it anymore, and it's what you felt when Daegan confronted you."

"No, that's not it. It's just a release. It builds up."

"Tell me the rest."

Jennifer sagged back in her chair and poured out the rest of the story in practically one breath. From the Dark Room, to the dinner date to his apartment after. Then she revealed the rules.

Her friend shook her head. "I knew Daegan would be tough, but damn."

"Tough?" She nearly choked. "Try insane if he thinks I'm changing my life for him. This is not what I agreed to."

"What did you agree to?"

"Not that, that's for sure." Jennifer shot from her seat and paced across the room. "I tried to tell him."

"Maybe you should start listening instead of telling him what you think you know." Eve crossed her legs and sat back. "And I'm not just talking about listening to him. How about what's in here." She pointed to her chest. "You push people away. You hide. Even when your clothes are off and Murphy has you tied in knots, you withdraw behind a shield. Do you even acknowledge your needs to yourself?"

She started to open her mouth and clamped her lips instead. She swore she wouldn't be the kind of person afraid to face the truth.

"What do you want, Jennifer? You say you don't want a Dom/sub relationship, yet you gave in to Daegan's requests with very little fight. There has to be some place inside, some instinct where it felt right, or you'd never have agreed in the first place. Then it got hard. Even then, you tried to run away, and you couldn't. Why is that? What stopped you from getting in your car and driving away? Dig deep, Jennifer. I know you've had a hard life, but this isn't about the past. It's about your future and what you want it to be. I can guarantee it will be hard at times. A Dom will bring you to your knees and make you look at things you never thought you wanted to. He'll see inside you to the very core of your vulnerability. That kind of intimacy can't be faked nor replaced with anything else. It's who you are. Don't be afraid to find out. Daegan is a powerful, dominant man. You have to decide if you can trust him enough to explore your needs."

She hesitated while Eve's words clicked into place. "I don't know what to say."

"You don't need to say anything to me. Think about it. In fact, stay here and take all the time you need. No one will bother you here."

"Thank you, Eve."

"Don't thank me yet. If you decide to go back, and I think you should, it won't be easy. Just stop thinking with your head and go with your heart. That's all anyone should ask."

With that, Eve opened the office door and walked out, softly closing it behind her. The sudden silence consumed Jennifer's thoughts. She wanted to rail against the advice her friend had given her. If she could stomp her feet and embrace the anger she'd used earlier to walk out Daegan's door, the whole situation would be a hell of a lot simpler. Instead, she went round and round with what was stopping her. She had a nice and simple life with work and the occasional trip to the club to work out her frustrations. Why couldn't that be enough?

It was all his fault. The Irish devil made her think of things not meant for her. An exchange of power. His control for her submission. His protection and guidance instead of her destructive emotions. Jennifer sighed. They needed to talk. Maybe there was more to this than she'd thought, and maybe there wasn't. How would she ever know if she didn't even try? So far her life had been one big fight, and she'd grown weary of it. The fight for love from people who should have loved her no matter what, the fight for freedom to survive without love, and the fight against an inner craving for something that often drove her to the brink of madness.

Rules made her balk. She'd never lived by any. Not really. Don't be late for school or work. Always be polite to strangers. Do unto others as you'd want done to you. The normal shit every kid learned growing up. But these rules—these were personal. Rules specifically designed for her. If she followed them, it would be the ultimate test. Jennifer's stomach tumbled.

No one had ever given her any rules...

CHAPTER 8

*J*ennifer shifted from foot to foot, biting her lip while she anxiously waited for Daegan to answer his door. Her stomach twisted every time she imagined the anger she'd face and what it would take to make up to him for walking out. There was always the chance Eve was completely wrong about him, and he'd refuse to see her again. Her fear and indifference was often mistaken for brattiness, and there were many Doms with no tolerance for such behavior.

The door eased open, and Daegan immediately filled the opening. Tall with broad shoulders, his body alone dominated the space around her. He angled his body so one hip rested on the door frame and placed him easily within her personal space. Something deep inside her tingled, reminding her of how he managed to make her feel without ever speaking a word. *Protected.*

Silence stretched between them as he clearly waited for her to say something. Jennifer swallowed past the lump in her throat and tried to speak. "I—I'm sorry I walked out." God, apologizing like that sounded so lame. She wanted him to step back and usher her inside, not make her do this in the hallway. Instead, his intense scrutiny and everlasting patience made her feel like she stood under a microscope.

"You scared me," she admitted.

"Scared is okay. Unfortunately, walking away isn't. If you aren't willing to talk through and negotiate any issues you have, then we shouldn't even bother with anything more."

Jennifer hung her head. Of course he was right. She'd behaved like an idiot. "I've never had a relationship before. I don't know how to handle it." Her voice broke.

With his big, strong hand, Daegan cupped the back of her neck and pulled her toward him. She burrowed into his chest and inhaled deeply. As usual, his familiar scent of wood and man made butterflies churn in her stomach. A deep yearning blossomed inside her. Even amid anger and pain he made her feel different. Less alone. Jennifer sighed, her breath fanning against the soft fabric of his shirt.

"We have a lot to talk about." His voice came out harsh, thready.

Jennifer jerked under his hand and peered into his eyes. An interesting mix of anger, regret, and desire stared back at her. Her stomach somersaulted. Maybe he would let her transgression slide. What a fool she'd been. Still, he'd come up with those crazy rules and then sprung them on her out of the blue. Never would she have guessed he'd plan to be so—so involved.

They'd have to discuss it, but the tension between them stifled her. "I'm sorry for leaving. I realize now it was a mistake."

Daegan threaded his fingers in her hair and toyed with the back of her neck. Her skin prickled under the pleasure of his touch.

"You should never sneak out on me like that. It's the act of a petulant child."

Jennifer fell silent. His words rubbed her the wrong way. She crossed her arms over her chest and glared. If he wanted petulant child, she'd sure as hell give it to him. "I'll have to try and behave."

Daegan lifted an eyebrow and tightened his hand

around the back of her neck. "Now would not be the ideal time to misbehave," he warned.

Instead of mouthing off to him, Jennifer took a deep breath and slowly exhaled. This wasn't why she'd come. "When you told me the rules, I freaked. Wrong or right, I couldn't deal. I'm sorry."

The look on Daegan's face shifted, and some of the tension between them eased. "We don't have to talk tonight. It's getting late, and I think we both need some sleep." He pulled her farther into his apartment and closed the door behind her. "Do you want to stay this time?"

She swallowed around a lump in her throat and nodded.

"Good." He grabbed her hand and pulled her to the bedroom at the back of the apartment. "You can stay here tonight." He led her into the now dark room where she could make out nothing until he turned on a bedside lamp. "I'll be just across the apartment in the master bedroom if you need anything."

The room suddenly seemed even smaller than before. "I don't understand. This isn't your room?"

A soft smile tipped the corners of Daegan's mouth. "No, love. This is your room."

For once, Jennifer found herself speechless. This was the last thing in the world she expected from him. She'd assumed that if he forgave her, he'd want to have sex with her. Maybe finish what they'd started earlier. At the very least they'd share the same room.

"Don't look so shocked. This isn't just about how quick I can get my dick in your cunt, you know. Not that I won't be thinking about it all night though." He eased away from her and quietly began undressing her while she processed his crude words. Arousal burned through her now that he'd made it clear she'd be alone tonight. She didn't want a bed by herself. She wanted a lover, dammit.

"I thought you want to—" She hesitated. "You know."

"Dominate you?"

She nodded as the last of her clothes fell to her feet.

"Domination isn't just about sex. Not for me. I want you in here because you don't deserve a place in my bed tonight. Your behavior earlier earned you a punishment, and this is what I've decided on. First, go stand against the wall with your hands over your head."

Jennifer's eyes opened wide. "Excuse me?"

His lips pressed into a firm line. "I know you understood me."

"But—"

Daegan grasped her elbow and steered her to the wall. "Stop trying to argue with me at every turn. You can either accept my decisions or gather your clothes and leave."

She bit back a gasp. "What are you going to do?" She couldn't help it. The curiosity got to her. Fear of the unknown controlled her tongue. Not that it stopped her from following his directions and getting into position against the wall as requested.

"You, love, need some discipline in your life. I think you try really hard to keep life on an even keel, but far too often it spirals out of control, and you don't know what to do. So you go to the club and stand in line for a flogging or a whipping from a stranger. Does that make you happy?"

Jennifer grasped for the words to answer him, to tell him he didn't know what the hell he was talking about, but she forgot everything when he pressed his weight against her buttocks and back, pushing her into the wall.

The hard muscles of his arms wrapped around her shoulders at the same time his big hands clamped down on hers. The work-roughened skin sent a tremble through her body. He was planning to spank her and then leave her in a room by herself. If anything, she should be livid, but instead her body shivered under his touch and moisture pooled between her thighs. "My life is too complicated for this."

"That's exactly the point. You worry, you hide, and you manage to forget you are a woman with needs by working too much. Until you can't stand it anymore. That's no way to live, love."

"You don't..." God, talking to him like this was about as effective as talking to a brick wall. If she told him she wanted him to stop, it would be a big fat lie. Hell, if he stopped now, she might die from the need of it. She'd walked out on him, and he wanted to punish her for that, and she wanted his discipline. Fucked-up or not —she did.

He must have sensed her acquiescence. Daegan eased away from her while his palm began to rub her buttocks. "You need this, Jennifer. I'd even daresay you want it."

His calm, even tone struck low in her belly. Her sex squeezed, and her racing mind began to relax. If she really wanted to end this, she could. The option would always be hers to walk out the door whenever she was ready. The problem she feared was that she might never be ready again.

His hand cupped her bottom. "I want you to stay in position and take the spanking you deserve. Trust me when I say that you are getting off light this time. Keep that in mind next time you consider disobeying me."

Jennifer moaned, a half-strangled sound that shocked her. What did this mean? No one had done this before when she misbehaved. Sure her parents admonished her when she pushed for their attention, but they never followed through on any of her transgressions.

She felt him step back moments before his hand landed on her ass hard. *Oww.* Stinging pain erupted along her right cheek, bringing her on her toes with the shock of it.

"I don't want this," she moaned.

"Yes, you do. Now settle back down."

Oh God, he knew.

He spanked her again across the other cheek, and then he did it again, and again. Each blow landed harder than the last, and she writhed at the rising throb of not only her ass but her clit as well.

Thwack.

The sound screamed through the room, bringing her total focus on him and his actions. The harder he spanked her, the more she wanted. Some of her fears began to crack under the onslaught as the throb between her thighs became unbearably insistent. *More, please.*

The next blow landed harder than all the ones before it. She danced on her toes and wiggled away from him without moving her arms in the slightest. The scent of her arousal filled the room, betraying her for the deviant she'd become. The urge to beg him to fuck her began to beat at her brain until clamping her mouth shut no longer worked. With every smack to her ass, a flash of heat zinged straight to her pussy. Her arms and legs began to shake, and her moans erupted as fast as his hand landed on her backside.

She never questioned why any of this turned her on. Pain always did. Although never quite like this. God, he had to know how he affected her. How desperate she was for him to take her. The knowledge that he'd yet to slide his cock between her legs and take his pleasure drove her mad. She'd never felt so empty and desperate to be filled in her life. "Please, Daegan," she begged. He ignored her plea and continued for five more painful swats. Her head buzzed until she felt faint, and the pain in her bottom began to turn numb.

He must have sensed her distress, because he stopped then, which gave her little relief when he stepped closer and the rough denim of his pants brushed across her flaming ass. She didn't miss the hard length of his erection he nestled between the split of her bottom. Nor did she miss the almost growl that rumbled at her ear.

"Yes, please." Her plea was barely more than a whisper that only she may have heard.

"I could take you now, couldn't I?"

"Yes, yes." She ached for him more than she'd thought possible. It didn't help he'd wedged his hand between them to stroke his fingertips across her heated and tender flesh. The excruciating pleasure undid her, but it was the weight of his body against her and his firm touches that made her realize he now possessed her. Whatever he wanted, she'd give him.

"Oh, Jennifer." He rubbed his face into her hair and neck. "You have no idea how much I want to."

"Do it," she pleaded. Desperation engulfed her. Jennifer pushed her backside into his hand.

The second he pushed away from her, she cried out. The loss of his weight left her feeling adrift. Until she heard the distinct sound of a zipper being released. She held her breath—waiting. When the smooth flesh of his cock head prodded her, she whimpered in relief. Finally.

Instead of entering her like she'd hoped, he pushed forward, only resting his dick along the seam of her ass.

"Do you think you've learned your lesson?" he asked.

"Yes. I know I shouldn't have walked out without talking to you. I won't do it again. Please," she whimpered.

"I believe you." He traced the curve of her breast and side until his hand halted on her hip. "Unfortunately for us both, you're not getting fucked tonight."

"What? No!" she cried. "Please, Daegan. I'm sorry."

He drew one last breath and pushed away from her. She heard his zipper go up and the rustle of him moving away from her. Tears threatened her, as did the need to touch herself. If he planned to leave her like this, she'd be forced to take care of her needs the minute he left her alone. A lone tear escaped and slid down her cheek. She wanted him. More importantly she'd wanted his forgiveness.

"Come over here to the bed." The faraway sound of his voice pulled at her, beckoned her to do as he said. Jennifer pushed from the wall and turned to face him. Their gazes met. From the determination she spied in his vibrant blue eyes, she decided to keep her mouth shut and obey. *Obey.* Really the word still sounded so foreign to her. Not that it was wrong or anything, just so unfamiliar. She crossed the room and stood at the edge of the mattress. With the arousal now simmering instead of burning her alive, she realized how exhausted she was from the long day. Had it really only been one day? Their night in the Dark Room seemed like ages ago now.

"Lie down on your back and raise your right arm over your head."

Automatically she started to question but stopped when he narrowed his eyes. Her decision earlier had been to return to him and give this a real shot, and that's what she was going to do. Jennifer crawled onto the bed and flipped over, positioning herself as he'd requested.

"That's a good girl." He moved to the closet and disappeared inside.

Her nerves jumped sporadically as she waited for him. What did he have planned for the rest of the night if he wasn't going to give her sex? When he appeared in front of her again, he carried a long length of black rope in his hands and wore a slight smile on his face. Daegan leaned across her and tied the rope to the bedpost before shackling her wrist with the leather cuff attached to the opposite end. "Pull your arm as far as you can," he instructed.

She tested her range of movement and even gave the rope an extra tug to see what kind of give his knots had.

While she'd have no problem moving around with the slack he'd left her, the connection to the bed seemed fairly solid. A slight edge of panic crept through her mind.

"I should have asked if you needed to go to the bathroom."

"I'm fine," she answered.

Next, he pulled the comforter from the foot of the bed and carefully covered her. He brushed the hair from her face, leaned forward, and pressed a chaste kiss to her lips. "If you need anything, all you have to do is call for me. I'm not a heavy sleeper, and my room isn't that far away."

Fresh panic sliced through her. "What? I'm staying here by myself?"

"Don't sound so worried. Another night alone will give you the time you need to consider everything that happened this evening without anything to interrupt your train of thought."

She jerked on the rope keeping her attached to the bed. "But why this? I'm not going anywhere."

"So you say." He sighed, settling down on the edge of the mattress. "I think there's still a good chance you'll change your mind." His voice lowered, "I don't think I could bear waking up to find you gone again."

Surprised, she looked into his eyes, her breath catching at the naked pain and vulnerability showing there. An ache deep inside her bloomed bright. *Need.* The depth of which robbed her senses. Her nipples tightened, and her pussy moistened. Her body responded to him even when her brain made no sense.

"Okay, Daegan." She tried to keep her voice even, but her words came out broken anyway.

"I'll be right through there if you need anything." He nodded toward the door. "I'll be back in the morning to set you free."

Her stomach lurched. Maybe she didn't want her freedom anymore. It seemed the more she let him in, the less she wanted to go back to the way things were. She still wasn't sure how she'd handle the job issue, but she was tired. Tired of the same old same old and tired of not believing.

"Good night, love." He brushed her lips with the tips of his fingers and stood from the bed. "Oh and Jennifer." He paused. "Apology accepted." With those parting words, he walked through the door, only stopping long enough to turn the light off. She heaved a sigh of relief when he left the door open. There was an odd longing inside her to keep some connection between them. Her body hummed with unmet need, something she could easily take care of herself. Instead she drew her legs into her chest and comforted herself with amazing images of Daegan punishing her and then putting her to bed. Yes, it seemed odd to get the warm and fuzzies about such things. She didn't care. She was alone in his guest room, but for the first time in a really long time, she wasn't lonely.

CHAPTER 9

*D*aegan leaned against the door frame and stared at Jennifer sleeping in the small bed. He'd tried everything to fall asleep, even going so far as to drink some warm milk to no avail. He palmed his hard erection, giving it a firm squeeze. *Hard to rest with this bloody thing getting in the way.* Not to mention the allure of knowing the woman he'd become obsessed with slept less than thirty feet from his door.

Obsession is a slippery slope.

Admittedly he'd waited too damn long to get back into the game. It didn't matter. What he felt for Jennifer was simply natural after Claire. Daegan blocked the image of his wife. She had no place in this. He deserved a respite from the grief, and the woman fighting him every step of the way provided just the challenge he needed to get past this.

Maybe he'd come on a little stronger than he'd intended, but she desperately needed some structure in her life. How many times had he spied the wild-eyed look of a woman out of control? Some subs didn't know how to ask for what they needed, making his job more difficult but not impossible. In the moment, his decision had felt right. He'd really enjoyed spanking her and judging by how needy and wet she'd become, he'd say she'd enjoyed it too. She responded to him better than he'd dreamed. Still, she had so many hesitations. That dichotomy aroused him, no doubt. It also worried him. He was getting too damned attached, and if she truly wasn't capable of making a commitment to the lifestyle, they were both going to end up hurt. Daegan sighed. His job was to prevent that as much as possible.

He scrubbed his face and backed away from her room. There seemed to be no way to get the seductive scent of her arousal out of his head. He took a step in the direction of her door. And another. His entire body throbbed with the need to feel her wet heat surrounding him. To cuddle against her soft skin and breathe in her scent.

Ah, fuck it. He'd tried everything to suppress the urge to bury himself inside her heat, and nothing worked.

Daegan crossed the room and pulled the twisted comforter loose from her limbs. She stirred but didn't wake. Curled on her side and facing away from him, the first thing he noticed was the red blush of her ass from her spanking. He groaned while climbing into bed behind her. His fingers grazed the skin of her waist and hip, tracing the faint trails of freckles that dotted her skin. Somewhere along the line she'd spent a lot of time outdoors, letting the sunshine kiss her pale body. He savored the silk-smooth flesh along the small expanse of her waist. His palm flattened, and he swore her stomach muscles jumped under his touch.

The urge to keep her like this as much as possible overwhelmed him. Her beauty should be marred by clothing as little as possible. No wonder she made such a fantastic fetish model. Not only was she comfortable in her own skin, she had an extraordinary figure that didn't fit the mold of every other model he'd seen. Her hips were a little rounder than most, but that only enhanced the heart-shaped appearance and provided more leverage for rope.

There was so much more to her than the model though. He'd witnessed many small details that pulled at him. The fear he often saw in her eyes when someone wanted inside, the helpless look she turned on him every time he made a demand. There was so much goddamned need wrapped up in a tiny package, bursting to get out. When she let down her guard, her submissive nature would demand attention. He planned to be there to give it to her.

With a soft touch, he swept his hand underneath her breast, cupping it. He savored the weight of it. She murmured in her sleep, making him smile against her shoulder. Warm. Sweet. His. At least for now.

The thought made him harden more. He rolled his eyes and breathed deep, searching for a semblance of control. His gaze wandered to the hand resting above her head. He considered for about half a second taking the time to attach the other one to the headboard as well and decided he didn't want to wait that long to be inside her.

He snaked his hands down her front to the tops of her thighs, where he stroked his fingertips between her legs. He cupped her mound. "Wake up, love," he whispered in her ear. He nuzzled her face and nipped at her skin until she moaned and eagerly spread her legs for him. Her back arched as his fingers slid between the slippery folds of her pussy to the heat awaiting him. They moaned in unison.

"Lift your right leg," he commanded.

She languorously complied. She might be awake, but sleep still held her in some form of its grip. No matter. He needed her too much to stop now. He reached behind him and fumbled with the nightstand drawer until he found the condom he'd been looking for. For a few seconds he released her to tear open the packet and roll it onto his cock. He shuddered at the desperation gripping him.

Daegan slipped his arm underneath Jennifer's knee and lifted her leg until he cradled it in the crook of his elbow. He inched forward until the tip of his shaft nudged her opening.

"I'm going to fuck you now, love." He didn't wait for an answer or a sign. He simply bucked forward and slid inside her with one smooth stroke. Sensation exploded in his head as the tight wet sheath of her pussy gripped him like a vise. For a second his vision blurred.

"Daegan," she gasped.

Dark, sardonic thoughts filled his head. "I think it's about time you start calling me Sir or Master."

Her muscles clenched around his dick in response. "Ohhh..." she moaned.

"Say it." He pulled back and thrust into her hard. A wave of possessiveness swept through him. Hot pulses squeezed his cock. Much more of that, and he'd lose his mind. She was so slick with her own juices he wondered what the hell she'd been dreaming about. When she didn't respond, he gripped the tendon at the curve of her neck with his teeth and bore down.

"Sir!" she screamed.

Oh yeah. The satisfaction from her response spurred

him to bite harder while he flexed his hips, surging deeper than before. With one hand, he gripped her hip for leverage and began a steady in and out slide. Easy at first, then he picked up the pace, making every hard thrust slam into her. She wriggled and cried out under the onslaught until he tightened his grip and fastened her into place. No longer could she move or control anything. Her whimpers turned to pants, and he swelled further. Every sweet sound from her mouth slid up his spine in a tremor of pleasure, turning him into a man possessed.

Seeking more leverage, he pushed his free hand under her shoulder and banded her to him with his forearm.

"Please, Sir. Oh God, Sir." She trembled against him.

"It's what you wanted isn't it? Now I've got you. You're mine."

A choked sob escaped from her. That simple sound made him crazy. He pumped faster and felt his orgasm rising. Not willing to go there without her, he angled his hips upward and began a rhythm of short spiky jabs aimed directly at her G-spot. She cried out in shock.

"You feel even better than I'd imagined." His fingers dug into her flesh, making sure she couldn't move an inch as he hammered into her over and over. Eventually, he had to give in to the pleasure. He released her hips, slid his hand to the slick folds between her legs, and swiped his finger across her clit. The resulting jerk of her body brought a smile to his face.

"That's right, love. Time to come." He pressed down on the hard nub and drove his cock deep. Her long wail was music to his ears and almost as much pleasure as the sensation of her muscles milking his dick when she came. Her body convulsed every time her muscles flexed until blood roared in his ears and light flashed before his eyes.

He thrust one last time and snarled as his cock jerked inside her, spilling his cum into the condom. White-hot heat flooded his senses as her spasms clutched and pulled at him until he'd gone dry. Daegan slumped across her back and fought to catch his breath before his heart exploded.

Somehow the intensity had gotten away from him, and he'd nearly fucked her into the mattress. He stretched backward and pulled her with him so she too could get some air. Reluctantly he pulled out and eased from the bed. He slipped into the bathroom and quickly disposed of the condom, cleaned up, and returned to the bed with a warm, wet cloth.

With a soft touch, he took his time and gently cleaned her. She remained still, not saying a word as he worked. "Are you okay?"

She turned to look at him, a soft smile on her lips, and

his heart tripped in his chest. Glassy eyes, flushed skin, and swollen lips gave her a well-used look. He stifled a grin. She probably didn't want to know how much he liked seeing her like this. He pressed a soft kiss to her lips, eliciting a quiet moan. His fingers trailed along her thigh, tracing a path from knee to hip. The jitters and nerves from before had at least temporarily disappeared. He'd have to do this to her more often. In the last several hours, he'd finally managed to lower some of the shields she clung to like a life raft. The more he stroked and petted her, the softer she became.

He pulled her into the curve of his body and nestled against her ass. "You feel incredible, love."

"I really like it when you call me that. It sounds so special," she murmured.

"You are special," he responded, while with his free hand he caressed a breast. Under his touch, her nipples grew taut. Always so responsive. He smiled.

"I'm really glad you came back."

Jennifer's stomach flip-flopped at his admission. "I had to. I tried to leave. I really did. But—but I just couldn't. I kept dropping my keys in the parking lot."

His arm wrapped around her stomach, and he pulled

her closer. So close she thought she felt the thumping of his heartbeat on her back.

"Don't be afraid," he reassured her. "We just need to get to know each other better, and then we'll figure it out."

She sighed. He didn't want to know her. Not really. No one wanted the dark parts inside her.

"I already know about your career and your extracurricular activities." He pinched her nipple.

"Hey," she halfheartedly protested.

"So tell me something I don't know. Tell me something about your childhood. Why have you been on your own since you were sixteen? Did something happen?" His hand stroked through her hair as she considered his question.

Deep memories she managed to keep hidden began to rise, and Jennifer squeezed her eyes against them. "Be careful what you wish for."

He pressed a kiss to her nape. "I can take it. Trust me. Where I grew up, it wasn't all picket fences and roses, you know. Ireland can be harsh when she wants to be, and no one is immune."

Jennifer took a deep breath. There was one memory that would forever remain ingrained as the moment she'd known for sure she didn't belong.

"When I was a child, I used to sleepwalk. I'd wander around the house, often holding complete conversations with my mom or dad while still fully asleep. It became a running joke in our family all the precautions they had to take to keep me in the house. Chimes on the doors. Special locks on the windows. All sorts of things like that." She snuggled into him, glad to have him at her back so that she didn't have to look at him as she remembered that awful night. "After a while they quit paying attention, and eventually I'd go back to full sleep. So one night when I woke to a man sitting on my bed and rubbing my leg, my father didn't come when he heard my screams. Everyone assumed I was having another night episode."

"Oh hell, Jennifer."

She clenched her hands. "No, don't. Please don't say anything, or I won't be able to finish." His grip around her waist tightened, but he refrained from saying anything else. The first tear fell at the faith he'd just demonstrated in her request.

"I was asleep in a room with my sister, and even she ignored the first few screams. It was so dark in there, Daegan. I couldn't make out much more than the shape of the man who kept trying to comfort and calm me. His hand continued to stroke my leg while he told me it was okay, that he was my father. But I knew it wasn't. It's funny how the strangest things occur to you

137

in a state of fear and panic. The only reason I knew it wasn't my father was because of his baseball cap. My father would never be caught dead wearing such a thing. It's the one thing that I saw clearly and kept me from accepting a stranger's word. Eventually my screams roused my sister, and when she saw the man sitting on my bed, she screamed too. That got my father's attention. And that of the man on my bed as well. He got up and left the room pretty quickly, but not before he told me that he'd be back for me."

Her stomach roiled at the horrible memory of that night. As much as she'd tried to forget it, she knew she never would. She moved past it and rarely thought about it, but it would never be completely forgotten. Ever.

"A few seconds later, my dad came rushing into the room with a baseball bat. Unfortunately both my sister and I were pretty hysterical, and it took several minutes to calm us down before we got the story out."

"Plenty of time for the asshole to get out of the house."

Jennifer shuddered against him. "Yes. My father found the front door open and immediately called the police."

"Was the guy ever caught?"

"No." If only the story ended there. "But don't worry; this story doesn't end with some creep snatching me later on down the road." No, as far as she was concerned, what happened that night was far worse than a stranger hurting her.

Daegan stilled behind her. She held her breath while the pain lanced through her and the tears burned at the back of her eyes. No way would she cry again. She'd shed more than her fair share over the years.

"What's missing?"

Jennifer exhaled nice and slow. "When the police came, they discovered the intruder had come in through my brother's window at the opposite end of the house. He slept under that very window. My step-mother freaked out and gathered my sister and brother, along with my father and huddled them together on the couch. She wailed that someone could have hurt her son or her daughter. My dad held them. They cried together, and he spent hours soothing them with comforting touches and a lot of hugs. Eventually they grew weary, and everyone went to bed. But my step-mother couldn't bear to leave her children alone, so they all slept together in my parents' room." Shame burned through her as she remembered. The deep sadness of that night pressed down on her again now. She didn't even realize she'd begun to cry until a tear rolled into her mouth and she licked it away.

"I don't understand. Where were you in all of this?"

"I was in the corner of the living room alone. No one

spoke to me. No one comforted me. And no one took me to bed. When the lights turned out and they left me there forgotten in the dark. It was then I knew for certain."

No one loved me.

"Jesus fucking Christ." Daegan lifted her and turned her in his arms until she was resettled facing him. He grasped both sides of her head and brought his lips tenderly to hers. "I don't even know what to say."

She shook her head violently trying to free herself from his grip. He held fast. "Don't say anything. It was a long time ago. The last thing I need now is for someone to pity me. Eventually, after three years of waiting and planning, I got my day in court. The judge must have seen something from my parents—who weren't fighting to keep me—he didn't like, and he signed emancipation papers with very little fanfare. I was a pretty smart kid. I finished high school early, so I already had a full-time job, and that made it a little easier to support myself. It was such a relief to get away from my family and their weirdness."

"Oh, Jennifer," he said. Two little words, and she had to fight to keep from crying again. The tenderness she spied in his eyes threatened to unravel her.

"Please don't feel sorry for me, I don't think I could take it. Anything but that," she whispered.

"It makes me viciously angry that someone would treat you like that and it makes me bloody proud that you overcame it. You built a life for yourself, a damned good one. But you've taken it as far as you can go on your own. I know you know this."

She resisted the tender way he spoke the strong words. Believing in them... Her emotions were too raw. She couldn't breathe or think like this. Jennifer squirmed in his grasp. "Let me go," she pleaded.

"I don't think I can." He nuzzled her cheek, making her senses flare to life. His warmth enveloped her in a safe cocoon, giving merit to the wild thoughts of safety and connection she felt with him. Her eyes fluttered closed, and she gave herself the freedom to imagine a future as a submissive to a very dominant man. The ache in her bottom from the ruthless spanking he'd given her and the snug cuff still at her wrist were near-constant reminders of just how demanding he'd be, a thought that aroused her instead of instilling fear like she'd expected.

"You're beautiful and stubborn. Reckless and wild. Now my job is to give you what you need to find that balance."

She sucked in a breath. Her brain could barely wrap around what he said. Let alone believe in it.

Daegan rolled her onto her back and rose over her. He

thrust a knee between her legs. "Spread your legs," he commanded.

"But you said—"

Foil ripped, and seconds later he slid inside her.

"Don't confuse needs for wants. I may or may not give you what you want. I will however, eventually know everything about you."

The deep tone of Daegan's statement shivered along her flesh. She'd told him something she'd never spoken aloud to another soul. The cracks in her walls were growing wider and this... This felt suspiciously like making love.

CHAPTER 10

Jennifer entered Altered Ego to find Eve in the midst of chaos. There were huge boxes nearly filling the reception area while she gripped the phone to her ear with murderous intent shining in her eyes. A harsh curse word sounded from one of the offices, and Jennifer winced. If Chase was in a foul mood, she had every mind to back out and come back later.

Before she could get away, Eve spotted her and waved her into the chair next to her desk. *Shit.* Maybe she should have taken Daegan's suggestion of a vacation and spent the week doing nothing more than catching up on some sleep and digging into some of the books she'd been meaning to get to. Or updating her neglected blog. She had several e-mails from fans who were anxious to hear about her glow-in-the-dark demonstration at the grand opening of the new and improved photo studio and art gallery.

Eve muttered something into the phone and then slammed it back in the receiver. "God, this is frigging ridiculous." She got up from her seat, stomped around her desk, and plopped down in a chair next to Jennifer.

The first thing Jennifer noticed were Eve's shoes. Monstrosities more like it. Black with tiny cherries all over them. "Holy shit. Are those five inches?" She motioned to the heels. The other woman's eyes lit up, and a huge smile broke across her face.

"You like? I found these online last week, and they arrived this morning." She flipped her feet from left to right, admiring the way they looked.

"I think I'd kill myself if I wore shoes like that all the time. It's bad enough when I have to wear them for a shoot."

Eve turned sympathetic eyes on her. "How are you taking everything with Daegan? Are you better now about not modeling anymore?"

Jennifer shrugged. "It's only temporary. He and I talked it out. Or more like he explained his thought process on it, and I've decided to try it. And just between you and me." She rolled her shoulders forward and back. "My body needs a break from the hours and hours of extreme bondage. As much as I love it, even the yoga exercises I do haven't been enough to ease the aches and pains lately."

Eve sat up straight and stared her down. "What? Why didn't you say something? I could have scheduled you for less work. If Chase finds out—"

"Don't worry about it. If I didn't want a job, I would have told you."

Her friend eyed her suspiciously before easing back in her chair. "Anybody ever told you what a stubborn ass you are?" Eve smiled.

"I may have heard it a time or two."

They both laughed. Jennifer didn't know what to make of it. She hadn't had any girlfriends to share with in too many years to count. Competition among models seemed to inhibit tight bonds, and she'd never even tried to get comfortable at the club. When she went there it was simply a means to an end—nothing more.

Maybe, just maybe, things were changing for her. She had an intriguing Dom anxious to work with her, and she'd agreed to expand her horizons with a temp job helping Eve with the Pleasure Playground. Jennifer ran her hand along the granite countertop while thinking about her options. When Daegan had shown her the model of what the Playground would look like when the project was completed, she'd been intrigued. Seeing it in 3-D had definitely put it into more perspective, and she'd begun to look forward to helping with its creation.

"Earth to Jennifer. Are you listening?"

Eve's insistent questioning drew her back to reality. "I'm sorry, what did you say?"

"I was talking about this stupid mess. All these boxes were delivered and dumped without so much as a by-your-leave before the delivery guys left."

"What's in them?"

"It's the fixtures for the jewelry store going in next door. It's supposed to be opened by next week, so I told Chase I'd get the basic layout of the store figured out before Tammy gets here on Friday."

"Tammy?"

Eve jumped up excitedly. "Ooh yeah. Wait until you meet her and get a look at her work. She makes the most glorious collars. She made mine."

Jennifer stared at the pretty red and black collar around Eve's neck. Her stomach tumbled. What would it feel like to be owned like that? To have Daegan collar her... *Whoa. Don't even think about going there.*

"It's very pretty."

"I think her shop will be the perfect complement to the art gallery. So we've got to get her space set up this week and start fielding some of these proposals from other vendors who've expressed interest in setting up a storefront in the Playground." Eve turned around and looked at the mess. "Sometimes I think we've bitten off more than we can chew."

"I think it's going to be incredible. A one-of-a-kind place that's for sure."

Eve beamed. "I sure hope so. Unfortunately, we've got a lot of work to do. Have I thanked you for taking on this position yet? I've been drowning for weeks, and I wasn't sure if Chase and Murphy were going to pull the plug on the project if I didn't get some help in here. They've been missing me." She winked.

"I bet." Jennifer wandered through the boxes, her mind calculating the work to be done in relation to the time frame. "What kind of proposals have you been getting?"

Eve turned to her computer and tapped a few keys and scrunched up her nose at the screen. "Let's see... I've got a few leather vendors, a bunch of toy stores, an erotic bakery, and even a hand-blown glass dildo vendor. Those are the ones that stand out so far anyway. We've already lined up the rooftop restaurant complete with outdoor play space, and I'm debating on a traditional club or an old-fashioned burlesque theater."

Jennifer raised her head on the last. "Oh burlesque sounds awesome."

Eve nodded. "I tend to agree. I want the Pleasure Playground to be really different, and I'm not sure adding a full-service club is the right direction to go."

"Yeah between Purgatory and Sanctuary, I think this town is covered as far as club space is concerned."

Eve swiveled in her chair. "See. That's exactly what I explained to Chase and Murphy, and they looked at me like I'd grown a second head."

Jennifer couldn't bite back her laugh. When Eve smiled, the moment grew infectious, and they both ended up giggling hysterically. For a moment, she began to believe that, yes, she might be making some progress. She'd never been all that great at making friends although she definitely wanted to. Somehow Daegan pushing into her life had a way of making her examine what she wanted going forward.

She wanted a life outside her career. Friends. A lover... The familiar fear pushed through her belly, fighting for control. Maybe she could learn. Daegan certainly seemed to have the patience she needed. With a lighter heart she said to Eve, "Well, Doms do tend to have a one-track mind sometimes."

"No kidding. Good thing mine have this place to keep them busy or I'd be tied to a bed 24-7."

They both smiled.

"How about I start with the space next door and start putting some of this stuff together."

"Are you sure?"

"Yep. What I can't handle on my own, we'll save for later when Chase and Murphy have some free time and can help move some of it around."

Eve heaved a sigh of relief. "That would be awesome. Have I mentioned how glad I am you're here to help? That Dom of yours may turn out to be a godsend."

Her Dom. It might take some getting used to, but she kind of liked the sound of that.

Hours later, Jennifer sat down on the floor and brushed some of the hair from her face. Sweat coated her skin, and she desperately needed some water. There was still a ton of work to be done, but the place was starting to look like more than an empty white box. Once she got some help with the placement of the counter and the cases, it wouldn't take her that long to finish pulling it together. Maybe one more day at the most.

Somewhere in the distance she heard the phone ring. Her muscles ached, and she didn't want to get up. Maybe Eve would answer it. By the third ring, she suspected her friend had disappeared elsewhere in the building. She hauled herself from the ground and made a mad dash for the reception desk. On the fifth ring, she grabbed the receiver and answered, "Altered Ego, can I help you?"

"Jennifer, is that you?"

Her blood turned ice-cold, and her heart seized. *Oh my God. No fucking way.*

"Yes, it is," she answered.

"It's Gwen." As if she didn't recognize the dragon lady's voice the second she heard it. She tightened her grip on the phone and fought the urge to hang up. Whatever reason her stepmother had found to call her could not be good.

"Hi." *What do you want now?* Acid burned in her stomach as she struggled with her composure.

"I am calling to let you know about your father. He's been ill. Not like you've bothered to call or keep up with him."

"What do you mean ill? What's wrong with him?" She ignored the witch's snide comments for now.

"It's his heart again. The doctor had to go in to break up a blockage. We almost lost him."

"What? Where is he now? What hospital is he at? Do I need to come home? Is he going to be okay?" Panic seized her.

"No, you don't need to do anything. That was last week. He's home now and recovering. But he could have died."

"Wait. What? Last week? Why didn't you call me sooner?" Her head began to throb. Her stomach heaved.

"I had no intention of calling you at all. You aren't part of this family, remember?"

Direct hit. Jennifer doubled over to catch her breath. In the blink of an eye she felt twelve years old all over again.

"You don't call. Not even on Father's Day. Why do you think you stopped getting Christmas gifts? If you can't keep up with your own father, then why should he bother to keep up with you? As far as I'm concerned, you'll never get anything ever again."

The hated tears her stepmother always invoked no matter how hard she fought slid down her cheeks. The last time she'd spoken to her dad, he'd pretty much told her that there was nothing he could do about his wife. *You should be used to her by now. It's time to just get over it.* Those words slid through her brain every time she thought about picking up the phone or going home for a visit. There was nothing she could do to change the past but, that didn't mean she had to live with it.

"Where is he now? Can I talk to him?" One more minute with this woman and she'd be ready to kill her.

"No, you cannot talk to him. I don't trust you not to upset him. I only called because he made me."

"Okay," she muttered. "I'm glad he's going to be okay." What was she supposed to say? Her stepmother was obviously spoiling for a fight, and Jennifer just wasn't in the mood to go there."

"I don't know why you bother to pretend to care."

At that exact moment, Eve walked back into the room. She laid eyes on Jennifer, and her face creased with concern.

"I've got to go now, I'm at work. Thanks for calling." She slid the phone from her ear and dropped it into the cradle.

"Oh my God, Jennifer. What's wrong? Has something happened?"

She turned away to hide the tears. "No, everything is

fine." She gripped her stomach and willed the meager contents to stay down.

"No, you are not fine. What happened?" She grabbed Jennifer's shoulder and tried to pull her around.

She couldn't stand here and take pity from her friend. Her stomach wouldn't take much more, and she needed to get to a bathroom fast. "I've got to go. I'm sorry. Everything will be fine. I just need a few minutes."

"Of course. Whatever you need. We've worked hard today, so you should go on up and see Daegan. He was looking for you the last time I saw him."

She flashed a quick look of gratitude to the other woman. "Thank you. Please don't worry, everything will be fine." Without waiting for a response, Jennifer fled the room and went for the nearest bathroom. Unfortunately the only restroom outside the photo studio was currently undergoing renovations. She'd either have to go back and face Eve, or go upstairs to Daegan's apartment. The key he'd tied around her neck earlier rested between her breasts. He'd wanted her to have a reminder of where she needed to be when she wasn't at work.

She'd found it an incredibly sweet gesture this morning. Now she grasped the key and held on to it like a lifeline. As quickly as possible, she ran for the stairs, taking them at a dead run. Her stomach continued to roil. In less than a minute, she made it to his apartment, whisked the key over her head and unlocked the door. A blast of cool air rushed over her when she got inside.

She didn't have much time. Dropping her key to the floor, she sprinted for the bathroom. Once inside she rushed forward, barely making the bowl before the heaving began and she emptied the contents of her stomach. For a long time after, the dry heaves shuddered through her until she collapsed on the floor. She rolled onto her back and stared at the ceiling. How did she let this crap happen to her? Not only had she escaped the fucked-up group she called family, she'd put an enormous amount of time and distance between them as well.

For the first time in a very long time she ached for someone specific to hold her. She'd give anything right now to have him curled around her naked body with his hands pinning her down. She needed.

Jennifer pushed to her feet and stared at herself in the mirror. Besides the red-rimmed eyes and the wild hair, she didn't look that much different from this morning. She quickly brushed her teeth, combed her hair, and set herself to rights again. No reason for Daegan to find her like this.

She wandered through his apartment for a few minutes, searching for any sign of him. When she found nothing, she stood in the middle of the living room and contemplated what to do. Her head ached. Her stomach felt ridiculously weak, and she wanted to cry again. Usually anger got her through one of these episodes, but the fact her father had been ill seemed to change everything. While she was relieved that he'd recovered, it devastated her to not be told until later. God, she hated that woman.

Without realizing what she'd done, Jennifer found herself back in the tiny room she'd slept in, staring down at the empty mattress. With her emotions now all over the map she wanted to embrace the memory of Daegan, no, her new Sir...new Master... She sounded them out, testing how they sounded. She'd stick with Sir for now. Master sounded so—so something more.

She'd felt safe here last night. More than that. Cared for.

Jennifer stripped her clothing and slid between the cool sheets, savoring the slight relief to her heated skin. Seeking more comfort, she curled onto her side in a repeat of last night. He'd left her alone and—Oh!

She lifted her head and spied the rope and cuff still attached to the bedpost. He'd shocked her when he'd tied her to the bed and then just left her alone. Although she'd not been alone at all. The sound of his footsteps outside her doorway had often reminded her he wasn't far. He'd been keeping an eye on her the whole time. He'd gone out of his way to make her feel safe even after she'd walked out on him.

The familiar burn of tears at the backs of her eyes prodded her to move. She grabbed the cuff and fastened it to her wrist. It didn't matter that she'd had the ability to get away if she wanted. The point had been he wanted her tied to the bed because he couldn't bear to find her gone again. Those words alone kept her company through a good portion of the night. Disappointing him again had not been an option. Now she curled into herself. She buried her nose into the sheets, drawing in a big breath and reveling in the mingled scents of them together. Her Sir.

The word came easier that time. She actually kind of liked it now. With his scent and her memories, she allowed the emotions to tumble free. Sobs tore through her as she released the pent-up frustration of her family once again getting under her skin. She slammed her fist into the pillow. This was ridiculous. She knew better than to let them get to her. When the tears dried up and her sobs became whimpers, a new sense of freedom settled over her. Here, cuffed to a tiny bed in an apartment in the middle of the day, a new sense of belonging settled over her.

With some of the fatigue of the day washed away, Jennifer slid her eyes closed and rested peacefully. She eagerly anticipated Daegan's arrival. He'd expect her to tell him everything about her day and somehow some way she'd figure out how to do just that. Whatever he wanted, she needed to give him. It was the least she could do for the comfort his actions had given her. Before she drifted off, she pulled her bindings taut and fell asleep with a clear mind and an open heart.

CHAPTER 11

"Come on in, Cathy. I wasn't sure you were ever going to come." He ushered his sister-in-law into his apartment and closed the door behind them. He glanced through the living room, grateful Jennifer hadn't returned. Shame burned through him.

"It's been a rough time for us all, but I guess now is as good a time as any to get this over with."

"I couldn't agree more. Why don't you have a seat, and I'll get the box for you. Would you like something to drink?" He hated the awkwardness of the situation, but having her here now didn't sit right with him.

"No, no, I'm fine. I really don't want to take up any more of your time than I have to."

"No worries. I'll be right back." He rushed into his bedroom and headed into the closet. It had been months since he'd contacted Cathy with the news he'd arrived in the States and that he had some personal belongings of Claire's that she'd wanted to go to her sister. Why the hell he'd never simply mailed them to her he had no idea. Her family had not approved of Claire relocating to Ireland when he'd decided to return home after college. She'd assured him that his wishes were her wishes, but her family had never forgiven him for taking her away.

He dug deeper into the closet, searching for the bloody box. He didn't really want Cathy to meet Jennifer. That meeting would probably not go well. He pushed past several bins full of clothing and a stack of magazines he really needed to throw away. In the corner he spied the box he wanted. He grabbed it and pulled it into his arms just in time to hear shouting coming from the living room.

What the hell?

He muscled his way out of the closet and burst into the living room to find Cathy standing in the doorway to the guest bedroom. She turned on him, her face red and contorted in rage.

"What is going on here?" She pointed into the room. "She is the spitting image of Claire, and she's chained to your bed."

Daegan's step faltered. *What?*

He rushed forward and looked over his sister-in-law's head to the confused sleepy face of Jennifer huddled in the middle of the bed and indeed shackled to the post in a repeat of last night. With her hair mussed from sleep and framing her face, he could see where Cathy might see a similarity.

"It's not what you think," he murmured. *Yeah it probably is.*

"What I think is you've gone and done the most disrespectful thing to my sister's memory you could. It wasn't bad enough you forced her into slavery until she died, but now you're on your way to doing it again with a look-alike."

"What?" Jennifer sat up. "Who is Claire?"

Oh hell.

Cathy turned on Jennifer. "Claire is my sister. His wife. He took her to Ireland and I never saw her again. Not until she died."

Daegan couldn't tell whether Cathy was going to pounce or disintegrate into a fit of tears. He needed to do something quick to defuse this situation.

"You're married? I mean were—I don't—" Jennifer reached for the cuff at her wrist.

"Don't," he ordered.

She swiveled toward him, disbelief in her eyes.

Cathy turned on him. "Give me the box so I can get the hell out of here. This whole situation sickens me. I should have listened to my gut when Claire first wanted to marry you. You've gone mad. Someone needs to do something about this." She grabbed the package from his hands and spun back toward Jennifer. "Run while you still can."

"Cathy, wait. You never understood."

"I don't want to hear your lies. What you're doing here with—her. It's disgusting."

Daegan found himself torn between trying to stop Cathy so he could explain and going to Jennifer who sat stricken on the bed. What the hell was she doing shackled to the bed anyway?

"Cathy, I'm sorry you don't understand. But if you aren't going to listen, then I'm not going to waste my time."

Her face darkened. "I'll report you to the authorities." She stomped to the front door. "One of these days, you will pay for this. I believe in karma, and you're going to end up in a world of shit for this."

She left the apartment, slamming the door behind her. Daegan rubbed his hand over his head and across his face. Good Lord, what a mess. This wasn't how he wanted to leave things with Claire's family. He had enough guilt to deal with as it was. Now he'd have to give them some time to cool off, and start again. He could never tell them that it was Claire who refused to leave him long enough to visit her family. She'd been possessed with the need to be by his side at all times. Even when she'd fallen ill, she'd worried only about him. No amount of coercion had changed her mind, and he didn't have the heart to go against her dying wishes. He glanced at the door one last time before making up his mind to consider Claire's family later. They were a part of his past.

In the meantime, he had a pissed-off sub tied to his bed, and he wanted to know why. He turned and strode to the bedroom. She'd listened to him and not undone the bindings, but the look on her face spoke volumes.

"I'm taking this off right now." She seethed.

He glared back at her. "No."

"What? You've got to be kidding me. That woman just—"

"I know exactly what happened, and you're going to listen to what I have to say. No more running, remember? In the meantime, I'd be reconsidering how you speak to me. I'm not feeling particularly generous at the moment."

Her eyes widened. She was pissed with good reason.

He moved to the bed and brushed her hair behind her ear. "Cathy blew that way out of proportion."

"I didn't even know you were married. That seems like kind of important information." She pressed her lips together.

"Scoot over." He watched her hesitate for a few seconds before finally deciding to obey. She shifted on the bed, and he sat down next to her. "Good girl."

"You still have some explaining to do."

He chuckled. "You're right about that. Although, I think you do too." He tapped on the leather cuff at her wrist.

She lifted her arm and cupped her wrist. For a few seconds something dark came across her face before she managed to get it back under control. Something had gone very wrong today, and he needed to find out what.

"How long has it been?"

She didn't have to specify; he knew exactly what she meant. "It's been a very long time. Long before I came here and met you."

"Please tell me she lied about me looking like your deceased wife."

Oh boy. "You resemble her some. Same hair color, same

E.M. GAYLE

body type, but it's not as close as Cathy would have you believe." He wrapped his hand around her free wrist and pushed her flat on her back. Rising over her, he watched her body language carefully. "Everything else is different. If Cathy had bothered to listen and spend five minutes with you, she'd have seen the differences. You are wild, untamed with a craving to submit you don't understand yet. You couldn't be more different."

"Why didn't you tell me? That kind of information seems, well... Important."

"I had planned to. Maybe even tonight." He pressed a kiss to her forehead at the same time he settled between her legs. "Claire is my past. It wasn't that pressing."

"I don't agree." Her words came out breathless. Obviously his position began having an effect on her.

"Point taken. Now tell me, love. Why are you tied to my bed when I didn't put you there?" He pressed his cock to the apex of her thighs. Her mouth formed a little O and her eyes grew wide. He nudged her clit.

"Daegan," she gasped.

"What?"

"I mean, Sir." She responded breathlessly. "I'm sorry, I can't think straight when you do that."

164

"Good. Now tell me."

"I—uh—I—I don't want to talk about it." She averted her eyes.

Daegan cupped her chin and pulled until she was forced to face him. "Did I ask if you wanted to talk about it?"

She didn't respond.

"I can't do my job as your Dom if I don't know everything that is going on with you."

"I'm not a job," she argued.

Things were going from bad to worse pretty quickly. "That's not what I meant, and I think you know that. I'm guessing something bad happened today and then Cathy—"

"It sucks when you're caught in a lie, doesn't it?" she spat.

He sighed. "Stop trying to use me as your excuse to escape. If you still have an issue with what happened, we'll discuss it like adults." He tightened his hands on her wrists and her expression immediately changed. Some of the anger slipped, and he saw the desperation underneath.

"I tried to tell you from the beginning I wasn't cut out for this."

"Don't bullshit me, Jennifer. Something happened today that hurt you. Badly enough that you came here and shackled yourself to the bed trying to find some comfort. Now I want to know why."

She started to protest.

"Don't. Fucking. Lie." He pressed her into the mattress with the full length of his body. She had no idea how close she was to getting flipped on her stomach and fucked in the ass. "There is nothing wrong with taking comfort in submission. What do you think you're doing when you go to the club once a month like clockwork for a flogging?"

"It's fun," she protested.

"Oh no doubt about that. But that's not why you seek strangers. It's all about easing the pain inside. I bet if I turned you over right now, spanked your ass red, and then fucked you into oblivion, you'd glow like a goddamned night-light."

She started to open her mouth and then quickly clamped it shut. *Smart girl.* He noticed the tears flooding her eyes and practically felt the inner struggle to hold them at bay. Poor baby. She needed him. Just as he needed her.

"There's nothing wrong with being controlled. The need to be safe is a common trait. I want to be the one in control," he leaned close to her face, "the one who gives you the discipline you need," he brushed his lips across hers until she shuddered underneath him, "the one who calms your racing mind."

Her body shook, a slight tremble. There wasn't a doubt in his mind that he was right. Not after this. She'd actually come full circle in a matter of days. It stunned him. He'd expected it would take weeks to get this far. He rained kisses down the curve of her neck and across the slope of her shoulder. "What happened, love? Did someone hurt you?"

After the story she'd confessed last night, he'd had to control the impulse to keep her close every minute. He'd thought of her often during the day. Soft skin and willful eyes filled his head.

"I got a call from my family."

His body stiffened and not in a good way. Muscles tightened in his neck to the point of pain. "Who called?" For some reason it mattered to him who she'd spoken to. The pain that led her to his bed had to run deep. This was the source.

"The wicked stepmother, of course."

The sarcasm of her delivery didn't hide the hurt in her eyes, no mattered how hard she tried. The small lines around her mouth and the sadness in her gaze spoke volumes her words didn't. "What did she say?"

"Do we have to do this now? I'm still reeling from your revelations to then have to get into mine."

Daegan compressed his lips into a frown. "Don't try to play me in this. The situation with Cathy is barely a blip."

"A blip?" Her voice rose. "Your lack of honesty is hardly a blip. I get that you're from a different country and all, but c'mon."

He growled deep in his chest. "I'm not going to keep explaining me self over and over, little sub. You entered into this apartment under a clear set of rules, so can the disrespect and tell me what she said."

Jennifer bit her lip, looking undecided whether to snap at him or not. He loved that internal byplay that crossed her face every time he made her uncomfortable. Years of independence and solitude struggled against the desire to let him care for her. She'd learn.

"Apparently my father has been ill, and now that he's recovered, she opted to take today as an opportunity to twist the ever-present knife in my back." She pulled her bottom lip back into her mouth but not before he caught the slight tremble. So much bluster.

"I'm glad your father is okay now." He'd heard enough about her family to easily understand why she stood apart from everyone.

"I don't know why I let her get to me so much. She used to regularly pull this crap with me until I knocked her down a few pegs many years ago. She caught me off guard is all. Hell, I didn't even think anyone in my family knew where I worked."

"You aren't like them, you know. You broke free from their narrow-mindedness. I can't imagine that was an easy thing to do, but you did it. You got a job as a fetish model, one who tends to mesmerize everyone, I might add, and you made a success of your life."

"A job you now won't let me do."

"Jennifer," he warned. "You agreed to this, and you're either in it or you're not."

Her teeth nibbled at her now plump bottom lip. "What do you want me to do? Please tell me. I want you to like me."

Daegan shook his head and released his grip on her wrists. Her face fell. He ignored her reaction and lifted himself from the bed. Good thing he had plenty of tricks up his sleeve. He retrieved a few supplies from the closet and dropped them on the bed. "Spread your legs."

Thankfully, she obeyed without hesitation. He grabbed one leg and attached a cuff to her thigh and then clipped it to the cuff on her wrist.

Her eyes grew wide.

He then added a pretty leather band to her free wrist and tied her to the opposite bed post. Daegan held out his hand for her other leg. With only a hint of hesitation she lifted and placed her ankle in his palm where he proceeded to cuff and attach it to the corresponding wrist restraint. With her legs bent and restrained, he had full and complete access to his lovely new sub without worrying about her fighting him. "This little bed is handier than I expected. Although it needs to be bigger.

"Bigger?"

"Oh yeah. We need more room than this for proper fucking."

She glanced around her and turned curious eyes his way.

"Just wait, love. There's much more to come." He took a few seconds to admire the pretty picture she made before he stood and stripped. He eased onto the bed and slipped between her legs.

"I've been waiting for this all day." He licked his lips. "Pretty pink pussy just for me," he whispered across her wet folds. "Wet too." He stroked a finger from clit to opening and swirled through her juices, then slid the tip of his finger inside her.

Jennifer moaned. "Oh, Sir..."

"It's time for a little torture," he warned with a wicked grin. He wasted no time, licking across her swollen clit repeatedly. Her hands struggled with her bonds. Unless she uttered her safe word, she had nowhere to go. Her eyes slid closed.

"Eyes on me, love. I want you to watch as I wring every ounce of pleasure from you that you think you can have, and then I'll give you some more."

She moaned again, her hips jerking slightly against his mouth. Her restraints offered her very little give. He alternately nibbled and sucked on the sensitive bundle of nerves until she struggled for breath. With teeth and tongue he tormented every nerve ending he could find. He eased his finger in and out of her cunt with precise movements designed to touch her G-spot on every thrust.

"Oh yes!" she exclaimed. "Please...please Sir."

She was responding even better than he'd expected. He added a second finger alongside the first and scissored his fingers to loosen her tight muscles. Everything about Jennifer appealed to him. Her sassiness challenged him, her easy responses drove him wild, and—he breathed deeply—her sweet, musky scent made him want to stay here like this for hours.

Her muscles quivered around his fingers, signaling he

needed to slow things down. He withdrew his fingers, ignoring her whimper of protest. His wet fingers slid beyond the opening to the smaller hole of her ass.

"Like that, love?"

"Yes," she wailed.

"Mmm. I can't wait to fuck you there." He slipped one finger past the tight ring. "So fucking tight..." He wanted to drag this out, but she'd been so good, all things considered. At this point there was no usefulness in punishing either of them. Their day had gone to shit, but together they'd righted things back to where they belonged. With a finger in her ass, he licked at the succulent flesh of her pussy. Up one side and down the other. Warm, silky flesh against his tongue made his dick swell with the need to be inside her, feeling the hot fist of her pussy squeezing him to release.

"Please, please," she begged. "I can't take it. I hurt."

"I know, love. Me too." He flicked across her clit, watching her eyes roll back in her head. Every muscle in his body grew taut. As close as she was, he wasn't far behind her.

"Come now, Jennifer," he ordered. He clamped her clitoris with his teeth and applied just the right amount of pressure to send her keening over the edge.

"Aahhhh."

The muscles of her anus clamped down on his finger, and he thought he might pass out from the pleasure of it. He quickly withdrew and grabbed a condom from his supplies on the edge of the bed. He tore at the foil and sheathed his cock. In one harsh thrust he impaled her, pushing through the convulsing muscles of her vagina.

Her screams tore through the room as she thrashed underneath him, her legs and arms pulling at the restraints. "Mmm. So tight, love. You feel so good." He managed to capture her lips for a kiss that muffled some of her screams. Her wet, tight sheath pulled at him rhythmically, more than enough to drive him insane.

He drove deeper, his balls slapping against the soft skin of her bottom. Yes, very soon he'd take her there and drive them both to the edge of their control. The sounds coming from her now were nothing compared to how she'd scream then. Mmm he loved that idea.

Jennifer whimpered and cried for more. She'd gone past pleasure after the first orgasm and now was suspended in an ache of need only he could satisfy. That knowledge filled him with pride. What an amazing woman she'd turned out to be. Despite the recklessness of her family, she'd gotten here all on her own. He'd only nudged her in the direction her instincts had tried to lead her.

The intensity of her heat around him grew too strong. His balls drew up, and the impending orgasm beat at his control. His cock swelled, triggering another orgasm from Jennifer. She spasmed so tight around him he couldn't take it anymore—he gave in to the pleasure engulfing him. He groaned into her neck and buried himself to the hilt, joining her in the incredible sensations.

CHAPTER 12

*T*he next morning Jennifer stayed in the bathroom much longer than she needed to. She stared at her body in the big mirror on the wall, turning to see all of the marks Daegan had left on her. Faint lines on her ass, a little chafing at her wrist, and a few minor bruises strategically placed here and there across her skin. No wonder he didn't want her to model. The man liked to play rough and with this many markings, she'd be useless at work unless Chase incorporated them into the shoot.

The morning after was still a new concept for her and would take some getting used to. Or maybe today seemed difficult because last night's revelations still taunted her. The pretty woman who'd found her tied to the bed had insisted that she looked exactly like Daegan's dead wife. *A wife.* She sat heavily on the toilet seat. Not that she didn't come with her own baggage from the past. She fleetingly thought of her unwelcome phone call from yesterday before shutting it out.

Why should she be so surprised he'd been married before? A Dom like him wouldn't be unattached for long. While she'd never sought any long-term attachments, she'd heard plenty of other women talk about what they were looking for. Sexual domination, structure, and on many occasions, discipline. Daegan had all of those things in spades. In the past she'd easily brushed any stray thoughts of more than club play from her mind and kept her focus on work. Until now...

Exactly as the bastard had designed. Without her work to act as a buffer, other things consumed her thoughts. Mainly Daegan and how he made her feel. She hadn't even thought twice about coming here when she'd been upset. He'd made it easy for her to turn to him and in his absence, she'd made do with a form of his control by using the restraint he'd left on her bed.

Her stomach fluttered at the remembered safety of it. The closeness she'd felt with Daegan... Jennifer shook her head and tried to break free from those thoughts. Was she crazy? Next thing she knew, she'd be replacing pleasure with love. Love. Her spine straightened. No fucking way. It had only been a few days since their night in the Dark Room. Nobody fell in love that quickly. Especially not her.

What about his wife? her conscience nagged.

Did she really resemble his wife? The thought made her stomach cramp. It would be bad enough to get attached, but it would be even worse to get attached to someone who was so obsessed with his dead wife that he was looking for a replica. He'd said it wasn't true. Blonde hair and body type could simply be a coincidence.

"Jennifer, are you all right?" Daegan wiggled the knob she'd locked behind her. "Why is the door locked?"

"Habit," she answered. That and she needed to be alone with her thoughts. She wasn't ready to talk to him yet.

"I've got a meeting this morning uptown. I have to leave soon."

"Okay."

"Jennifer. I don't like this. We shouldn't be having a conversation through a door."

"I'll be out in a few minutes. If you need to go ahead and go, I understand." Torn between running into his arms and hiding out in the bathroom, she hoped he'd let it go.

"Jennifer," he growled.

No such luck. On a weighty sigh she gave in and went to the door, unlocked it, and peeked out. He stood scowling in front of her. Before she could say anything, he pulled her into his arms and banded her tight against him. "You're acting like my jackrabbit. So skittish. What's wrong?"

She pressed her nose into his chest and shook her head. This wasn't the time to get into it.

Daegan wrapped his fingers in her hair and tugged her head until she lifted her gaze to meet his. "You're so stubborn. Almost too much." He bit at her lip, sending a sudden shiver of sensation through her body. "Do you always fret this much?"

"I'm not—" He covered her mouth with his and seared her with a hard kiss. His tongue pushed past her lips to slide against hers until she moaned in response. He touched her breasts and cupped her ass, making her forget what she'd been so worried about. He made it impossible to keep a level head in his presence.

His touch picked up tempo, and she pushed against the immovable wall of his chest. "You have to go."

"I have time." He began undoing his pants. "You need this."

She shook her head in denial, waiting for him to call

her the little liar she was. Instead he pulled a condom from his pocket and rolled it on. The immediate heat and wetness between her thighs would give her away the instant he touched her.

"If I didn't have a meeting to get to, you'd be on your knees sucking me first."

"But—"

"Enough. Stop talking now."

She managed to hold her tongue, but the groan of need slipped unbidden from deep within her. Why bother protesting? She wanted him so bad it hurt.

He wrapped his arms around her waist and lifted her from the ground. "Wrap your legs around my waist, love. If you spent half as much time feeling as you do thinking, this wouldn't be so hard for you."

She locked her legs behind his back and sucked in a sharp breath when the head of his cock probed at her wet folds.

"See? Hot and slick gives you away every time." He lowered her onto his shaft, impaling her one slow, sweet inch at a time. Her tissues stretched to accommodate him, giving her a sense of fullness that made her head spin.

"Ahh," she moaned. Sex had never been like this. She grabbed on to his shoulders to steady herself while his hands cupped the globes of her ass. His fingers dug into her flesh seconds before he thrust into her—rough. When she attempted to lift her hips, he growled, "I don't think so." He tightened his hands and drove harder.

Helpless to do anything but feel, she squeezed her fingers, digging her tiny nails into his skin. Every new stroke sent shocks of pleasure careening through her system. On a hard thrust, he pushed her into the wall and released one ass cheek. He rolled and pinched a nipple between his fingers to hard, painful points. Under the onslaught of sensations, all her reservations fled her mind, leaving her a writhing mass of hungry need.

"Please, Daegan."

"Look at me," he ordered. She was so close she couldn't think straight. "Dammit, Jennifer. Look at me." He nudged her face, forcing her to lift her head. "Ask me properly, and I might say yes."

"What?" Realization dawned as soon as the word left her mouth. Instead of admonishing her like she'd expected, he thrust harder inside her, taking care to drag his cock across her clit on each stroke. "Please, Sir. Make me come," she whined.

He pressed against her clit, making her whole body go rigid and taut. Her muscles clenched around him.

"Come now, love. Hurry." He stroked deep and fast inside her. She thought she felt him swell.

Bright light flashed in her head, shooting skyward as her climax seized her and sent her careening into the nothingness. Her body jerked uncontrollably several times, dragging him over the edge with her. He came on a shout, hard and fast, his balls slapping her flesh. He buried his length inside her, pushing her tight against the wall and barely giving her space to breathe.

Shuddering from the shock waves of pleasure, she wrapped her arms around his neck and held on for dear life. Emotions roiled through her, out of control. Underneath the fear threatening to drown her, she heard the steady rhythm of his heartbeat. She nestled closer and focused on the cadence of his breathing. He'd practically dragged her out of the bathroom and fucked her against a wall. Hot, fast, and dirty, and she'd loved every second of it.

What was happening to her?

"Don't do it, love," he murmured against her ear.

"What?"

"Don't try to analyze what just happened. I needed to have my stubborn sub, and I did. I only wish I had more time."

How much time did he want exactly? A week? A month? Forever?

Those thoughts left her scrambling to get out of his arms. Common sense overrode the crazy thoughts he planted in her head. No matter how hard she tried, she didn't know how to be what he wanted.

Daegan let her go on a sigh. Once on her feet, she longed to find something to cover up with. She started for the bed until a hand at her wrist stopped her.

"We shouldn't have done that." There wasn't any other way to say it.

A dark cloud passed over his face. "And why the hell not?"

"It's getting too complicated. I'm not a replac—" She barely stopped before the word came out. Although from the expression on his face, it was already too late.

"Jennifer," he warned. "Be very careful what you say next."

"Why? Am I right? Will you punish me for that?" She wanted to bite back the words. This wasn't the rational way to deal with this.

"Is that what you want me to do?"

"Of course not."

He lowered his face till their noses practically touched. "Little liar. Still afraid to accept what you want."

Torn between shoving him away and dropping to her knees, she ducked under his arm and slipped free from his grasp. "Like you said. Now is not the time for this. Don't you have a meeting to get to?"

She grabbed her shirt from the floor and tossed it over her head. "I don't have any more clean clothes. I need to go home this morning before I report to duty with Eve." A shower in her own apartment sounded heavenly at the moment.

Daegan glanced at his watch. "Unfortunately, I do need to go." He kissed her cheek. "I'll call you later. We're definitely not done here."

"I don't know..."

He tilted her head until their gazes met. "We are not done. Isn't it about time we both stopped running?"

Tears welled in her eyes. Dammit, why did she always have to cry? She had a reputation at the club of being frigid, yet she cried all the damn time. It was ridiculous.

She gave him a slight nod. "Fine," she whispered.

He chuckled. "So stubborn." He pressed another kiss to her lips. "Play nice today."

CHAPTER 13

*D*aegan headed to work with an optimistic outlook despite the reservations still plaguing him. Jennifer had slipped into the role of submissive with such ease, even she hadn't noticed. It chapped his ass that Cathy was the one who had found her tied to the bed instead of him. His little sub's need to find comfort in his restraints made his dick rock hard every time he thought of it.

Unfortunately, when he thought about why, a darkness spread inside him. Her family pissed him off. Why anyone in their right mind found it necessary to be so cruel to another human being made his head hurt. He was certain if he knew all the details of the phone call she'd received, he'd be on his way to Florida right now, not a meeting uptown. A fierce need to protect her washed over him. She deserved to be cherished and cared for. He shoved his fingers into his hair and scrubbed his face. Was he getting too close? Jennifer's needs were rooted in her past with a deep-seated desire to love and be loved. Not that she accepted that.

He couldn't take another repeat of Claire. If Jennifer didn't have a handle on her submission, how far would he be expected to take her? He didn't want a slave. He loved that Jennifer had a career and had no intentions of interfering once they got beyond the walls she built around herself. He laughed. Not that he'd have any trouble pulling her back if she got out of hand again.

There was no shame in needing or needing to give discipline. He relished the idea of setting rules and protocols that would keep her naked and ready any time they were together. But for the most part he simply wanted her sexual submission. If she butted heads with him on occasion, all the better. He wanted the challenge.

Claire had gone so deep in her role as his slave, he'd spent every waking moment dealing with every detail of their lives. From the time she woke up to the time she went to bed, he had to plan every minute for her or she'd curl in a ball and accomplish nothing. Over time he'd gotten tired and begun to dread going home.

Guilt ate away at his stomach like an insidious acid every time he remembered their life. She was his wife, whom he'd vowed to love forever, and all he could remember was the bad. No wonder Cathy hated him so much.

He doubted Jennifer would stay with him if she knew the whole truth. He'd been reluctant to mention his wife because if she asked for the details, he'd give them. Lying about it simply wasn't in his nature.

Stop.

He needed to keep his attention on Jennifer and what she needed. Her past didn't preclude her from a happy future. She only had to learn to believe. Her heart and body needed to overcome her brain. No matter how much she resisted him, when he took control and gave her orders, she melted every time. Hot, slick, and needy. The depth of her arousal pulled him in, giving them both the outcome they were looking for. It was a yin and yang type of thing. They fit. God, did they ever. Even now thinking about how hot she became when he fucked her made it bloody hard to concentrate on his work. For the first time in a long time she gave him something to look forward to besides a job.

What then? If they continued to enjoy each other, and he coaxed her from the hard shell she withdrew in. What then? When this job was over, would he simply help her find a permanent Dom and return to his old life in Ireland? He could return to his old routine and find a nice sub to serve him when he needed it. The thought didn't entice him at all. She'd slipped under his skin and getting over her would take some time.

Daegan tried to imagine another Dom touching Jennifer, tying her to a bed, and sliding his dick into her sweet cunt. He rose from his chair. *Mine.*

His gaze swept his desk. There was a pile of paperwork he had to get to. The day was slipping away, and he needed to focus and finish. He wanted to spend all evening with Jennifer, and that wasn't going to happen if he didn't get his head out of his ass and concentrate on the job. They'd have all night. And what a night it would be. He needed to explain Claire. But first there was a matter of some punishment.

The end of the day came and went without so much as a break for Daegan. It wasn't until the sun went down that he realized just how late it had gotten. He picked up his cell phone and called Jennifer. She didn't answer. With a frown on his face, and a bad feeling, he left his office and headed down to Altered Ego. There was still a chance she and Eve had worked late, and he'd find her amid empty boxes and paint cans. He stepped into the cool interior of the new jewelry store and stopped in shock at the transformation. Two days ago when he'd signed off on the go-ahead to begin setup, he'd left them with a blank white square. He turned to one side and then the other. The walls had been painted a deep blue color with some of Chase's amazing photography hung strategically around the room. One picture of Jennifer caught his eye, and he moved closer.

With her position on the couch, her face wasn't visible, although he knew exactly who it was. He'd studied her enough to know every inch of her. The smooth lines of her delicious body were only broken by the bright red color of the rope she'd been bound with. Chase did have a way with black and whites with a small splash of color. What the picture didn't show were the small smattering of freckles that trailed along her hips and thighs. Every time he saw them he wanted to lick his way from top to bottom.

Daegan shifted his stance, seeking relief from the hardening cock against his zipper. How bad did he have it when he got incredibly horny from a picture of his sub? His sub. He had to admit he really enjoyed calling her that.

"Can I help you?"

Startled, he turned toward the unfamiliar voice and came face-to-face with a pretty brunette. "I was looking for Jennifer. It appears my wayward sub has gone missing."

She blinked in apparent surprise. "You must be Daegan." She held out her hand.

He grasped her fingers. "And you are...?"

"I'm Tammy. This is going to be my new shop."

Of course. The jeweler. He'd heard she'd arrived early. Several of his crew had been out of their mind with discussing her at lunchtime. From the curly hair to the round, curvy figure he should have known, because she matched their description perfectly. Now he understood why the men were so enamored.

"Well, welcome Tammy. Everyone has been looking forward to your arrival and the new shop opening."

"Oh my goodness this is so exciting. I've never heard of a place like this before. I think Eve's idea is going to be a wild success."

He smiled at her enthusiasm. "I couldn't agree more. Chase and Murphy are going to have their hands full with her." For some reason his mention of Chase and Murphy made her flush bright red. The tinge of pink looked good on her. Her Dom must enjoy spanking her quite a bit. Speaking of...

"Have you seen Jennifer?" He was getting anxious to get his hands on her.

"I'm pretty sure she left a while ago. Maybe an hour or so."

"Okay no problem. She's probably already upstairs. Thanks for the help, and it was great meeting you."

"Likewise."

Daegan hightailed it up to his apartment to find it quiet and empty. This wasn't exactly the way he'd planned their evening. He'd hoped to settle her reservations once and for all so the rest of the night could be devoted to progressing Jennifer's submission. With her sudden disappearance, he had a feeling she was testing him. Not that he blamed her. Finding out about his wife from someone else had shaken her pretty badly. He'd give her a little more time to stew and then he'd find her and he'd spank her until she understood the truth.

With his decision made, he proceeded to take a shower and wash away the grime of his day. After two hours went by, he left the Playground and went looking. He tried her apartment first, but when he found no one home, the unease grew in his chest, giving him a solid idea of where she'd gone. Daegan fought the rising anger to no avail. That she'd gone to the club without him burned like a betrayal in his stomach.

Ten minutes later, he pulled into the parking lot of Purgatory and killed the engine of his car. He didn't have to search for her car; it stood out like a fucking beacon in a sea of dark SUVs. He was going to kill her.

Inside the club, he stood to the side of the entrance and allowed his eyes to adjust to the dark interior. Music thumped from speakers surrounding the main floor of the big room. He didn't even bother checking the dance floor. His wayward sub would be on the second floor where the play stations were located. When he reached the stairs, the club manager, Gabe, blocked his path.

"You're looking a little pissed tonight, Daegan. What's going on?"

"Let me pass. I'm looking for someone."

Gabe shook his head. "Now that definitely doesn't sound like a good idea until you calm down, my friend."

"I'll be perfectly fine just as soon as I find my sub." He started to push his way up the stairs.

"Ahh. I'd heard you and Jennifer had come to an agreement. Although I have to admit it came as a total surprise. I'm not sure I've ever seen a more reluctant sub in my life."

Daegan stopped and eyed Gabe warily. In the short time he'd known the man, he'd learned he had an uncanny ability to read people. "I don't think you understand her. Sure she's complicated, but underneath all her bluster she's soft and far more fragile than anyone realizes."

Gabe snorted. "I can't say fragile is a word anyone's used to describe her before."

The implication that he'd discussed his sub with other Doms annoyed the hell out of him. Despite the anger, all of his protective instincts rode close to the surface, and it wouldn't take much to provoke him. "Trust me, I know."

The other man narrowed his eyes. "Are you sure about that? You seem like a good guy, but Jennifer has been a member here a lot longer than you have. If you aren't willing to finish what you've started, then I think you should walk away now before it's too late."

The warning burned in Daegan's mind. "I appreciate that your job is to protect the members here, but this time you're wrong. I know exactly what I'm doing."

Gabe studied him for a minute more before letting his guard down. He stepped to the side and swept his arm in the direction of the play area. "Then I suggest you check out the flogging station first." With that, Gabe disappeared into the crowd and left him to stand and gape. With a last glance into the sea of people, Daegan pushed his way upstairs and into the overflowing play area. People were crammed into every available inch, making it difficult to see the flogging station. The sound of a whip cracking screamed through the air, accompanied by a few gasps and a delicious cry of agony when the leather tip hit flesh.

A few people glanced his way and immediately moved out of his path. When he got through enough of the crowd, what he found boiled his blood. Jennifer was being strapped to the St. Andrew's cross by a dark-haired sub. The attendant at the station plucked a flogger from the wall and made his way toward his sub.

Mine.

"Touch that flogger to my sub's skin and you'll not be able to wield it again for a week," Daegan growled in a low voice.

Several people behind him sucked in sharp breaths, and the area around him turned quiet and still except for the music coming from downstairs. Even with clothes covering her body, Daegan saw Jennifer's back go ramrod stiff when she heard his voice. 'That's right, love. Busted."

The man glared at him for a few seconds before he took a step back. He twisted the implement in his hand and offered Daegan the flogger. A dungeon master pushed through the crowd. "What's going on? Is everything okay?"

"I need some scissors," Daegan said.

The DM ignored him and repeated his question to the attendant.

"He claims this is his sub, and I'm guessing by the look on his face she didn't get his permission to do this."

The man walked to Jennifer's side "Is this true?"

A few seconds ticked by before she nodded her head. The tension among the crowd grew palpable. She'd just damned herself to a very painful or public punishment.

The DM approached him. "Do you want me to bring the punishment box?"

"Not yet. I need a pair of scissors or a knife," he repeated. "After, you can bring the box."

The DM's eyes grew wide. "As you wish, Sir."

Everyone stayed rooted in place until one of the young women from up front arrived with a pair of scissors. The DM placed them in his hand. "You do remember the rules of the club, right? No blood."

Daegan nodded and took the offering. He stalked toward Jennifer until he was close enough to touch. He wrapped his fingers around the back of her neck and bent toward her ear. "Have you ever heard the saying be careful what you wish for?"

She nodded.

He opened the scissors and sliced one side of her top open. The crowd behind him gasped. Oh they had no idea. She'd triggered the sadist inside, and he had every intention of making her beg for everything tonight. He continued to cut away her clothes until she lay against the cross—naked and exposed. She'd uttered not a single word of protest, and he'd lay money on how aroused she'd become.

"Do you remember your safe word, Jennifer?"

"Yes, Sir," she whispered on a shaky breath.

"Good. You might need it."

CHAPTER 14

*J*ennifer gulped for air. She'd never intended for things to get this far when she'd left the building after work today without letting him know. Her original idea had been to go home, have a really strong drink and then stare at the television until she got her head on straight. Instead, she'd started to analyze everything Daegan had ever said to her. Looking for clues to his deceit. She'd needed to find a reason not to trust him. When she'd gotten to the point she wanted to pull her hair out and scream in frustration, she'd grabbed her keys and purse and headed out for a drive.

Instead of the open road she'd thought of, she'd found herself in the crowded parking lot of Purgatory. Immediately the lure of the sights and smells of leather and sweat flashed through her memories, leaving her helpless to resist the call of pain. Like an endorphin junkie, she'd convinced herself in minutes that one little session on the cross wouldn't hurt. She didn't even have to take off her clothes. There was nothing wrong with that. It wasn't even a sexual thing.

Oh how she'd lied out her ass.

Cool air brushed across her heated skin, bringing her thoughts back to the situation at hand. Her pussy throbbed in anticipation. Until she remembered the look in his eyes. The disappointment he'd shown her despite the anger laced in his words.

"Why are you here, Jennifer?" he asked.

"I don't know."

"Lie." A sharp smack landed on her ass. Bright pain bloomed across her backside. Tears sprang to her eyes. That wasn't a flogger. He had a crop.

"Why are you here?" he repeated.

"I—I—needed some time to think."

Another smack landed on her right cheek. "That's not why you are here. Why are you here in the club, strapped to a cross?"

She started to process.

"Don't embarrass yourself with another lie. You don't have to come to a club to think. Why are you here?"

She swallowed, her hands tightening on her restraints. He was going to force her to admit everything in front of an audience. "I was looking for a brief escape. I thought about the pain..."

She jerked and went up on her toes when his evil crop landed on her left cheek. Another slap of leather, and her ass began to feel like it was on fire.

"The last I checked, you and I were in the midst of an agreement. Is that incorrect?"

"Yes. I mean no. It's not incorrect," she admitted.

"And you assumed coming to a club unescorted and without permission would be permissible?"

"I—It wasn't—"

Another sharp, fiery sensation streaked across her buttocks.

"Answer the question."

"No, Sir," she whispered.

"Much better." He rubbed the fiery stripes on her ass with the rough palm of his hand. "I'd call that act of defiance one of extreme disrespect, wouldn't you agree?"

"Yes, Sir." Several blows landed on her backside. She whimpered and cried out for each strike. It hurt like fucking hell, but with each touch of that little piece of leather, something loosened inside her. He was disciplining her. All she had to do to make it stop was say her safe word. She trusted Daegan to stop immediately if she did. She never came close to uttering it. Instead, each swat made her feel better. This was what he wanted from her at the moment, and she needed to submit to it. Something dark and heavy inside her unraveled and began to fade. The further she slipped under his will, the easier the pain became.

"This discipline is what you came for isn't it? You didn't think you could get what you needed from me so you came here." The deep tone of his voice unnerved her.

"I didn't know," she cried.

"And that, my love, is called topping from the bottom." He threw the crop against the wall, and she watched it bounce and land on the floor. She wanted to cry out and beg him not to stop. Not yet.

His hand grabbed the back of her neck. "Do you even know what the difference is between my discipline and some stranger beating your ass?" he snarled.

She shook her head, her legs trembling.

"I don't discipline you just because I get off on watching you tumble into headspace with tears in your eyes. I punish you because I care. Because making sure that you get what you need means the world to me."

Jennifer choked back sobs. Things were so fucked-up, and she didn't know how to fix them.

He released his hold and stepped back. "You can bring the punishment box now."

Stark fear surged through her. Many nights she'd watched a submissive subjected to the punishment box after breaking a club rule. She'd sworn that would never happen to her. She turned in time to see Gabe step onto the dais with the small box in his hands. This wasn't at all what she'd expected to happen tonight. Good God, what had she gotten herself into?

"You have a choice, Daegan. Either I can draw a card from the box, or you can take your sub and go home. In light of everything, you'd only be suspended for two weeks."

"No!" she screamed. All eyes turned to her in shock over her outburst. "I'm—I'm sorry. Please, Sir. I will take whatever punishment they see fit."

"Jennifer, that's not your decision to make," Daegan reproached.

"Please. Please, Sir. Let me do this for you. I'll do anything." The fact she meant every word she said surprised her. Suddenly her doubts about him faded, and she realized what a horrible judgment she'd made against him.

"Mmm. I had no idea your sub had begging in her."

Daegan frowned at Gabe before turning back to her. He stared hard at her, and she put every ounce of sincerity in the look she returned. She feared that saying anything else would not go well for her, but somehow she needed him to know how important this was.

"All right. Since this seems to mean so much to her, go ahead."

Gabe nodded. He set the punishment box on a bench and made quite a show of opening it and withdrawing a card. A hush fell across the crowd still watching everything as they all waited to see what fate had in store for her. The club manager glanced at the card without giving a hint of what it said. When she thought she might pass out from holding her breath, Gabe finally spoke.

"The chamber."

Oh shit.

The crowd roared its approval, and some even broke out in cheers. Jennifer took a deep breath and ignored the roaring of blood in her ears. She'd seen firsthand several times how utterly harsh the chamber could be. As far as she could tell, its sole purpose was to push a sub beyond all thought and into a place where they lost all inhibitions while on complete and total display. She shuddered with the image.

You can do this. You can do this. You can do this.

She had fucked up on a grand scale. For once in her life it wasn't going to be all about her. As in what can he do to her or not do to her, but what the hell could she do for him to make up for this shit storm she'd created. While he kept his expression blank, she well imagined the hurt and anger rising inside him. She'd gone out of her way to embarrass him. Even if that wasn't exactly what she'd intended. These were the consequences, and deep down she needed to bear them.

Gabe glanced at Daegan, apparently waiting his response. He nodded his head. She heaved a sigh of relief. As much as she hated the thought of the chamber, she feared him walking away from her far more. Not that she didn't deserve it at this point. When Gabe started toward her, she closed her eyes and concentrated on her breathing. Old fears had no place here tonight.

He unfastened her left wrist before crossing to her other side to undo the right. He leaned in where no one could hear.

"You have a safe word, Jennifer. Don't be afraid to use it. No one is going to blame you if you safe word out of this mess."

She shook her head. "No. Please just let me get it over with." She choked back the sobs threatening to burst free. "I have to make this right. Please let me."

Gabe thought for a moment, and she held her breath expecting him to put an end to her night.

"Very well. But if I think you're not being safe, you won't just be suspended for two weeks."

She blinked at the harsh words. "Yes, Sir," she responded.

He pulled her off the St. Andrew's cross and turned her to face the crowd. The heat of a violent blush swept through her body for probably the first time in too many years to count. She'd been seen far more explicitly than simply standing there by thousands of people over the years, so her embarrassment now made no sense.

From the wall, Gabe retrieved a collar and leash and proceeded to fasten the thick leather around her neck. The *click* of the leash connecting to the large D ring on the front of the collar boomed in her ears.

"Follow my lead, but stay at least three paces behind me," Gabe instructed before he started forward. When she stood rooted in place, he yanked on the chain and propelled her to move. Feeling way out of her league but knowing full well the protocols expected of her, Jennifer dropped her gaze to the floor. When she cleared the crowd in the play area, the music came to a screeching halt and a bright spotlight illuminated her. She stumbled, and hard hands grabbed her arms before she slammed into the floor.

Beautiful tanned hands, roughened from all the hard work he did remained wrapped around her biceps. She looked up into his hooded eyes. Save for the muscle tick in his jaw, he didn't look affected at all. "Be careful, love," he whispered.

"Yes, Sir." She looked back at the floor and watched her steps as Gabe led her around the club on full display. This little ritual was an added bonus for any sub lucky enough to get punished in the chamber. She sighed. Sarcasm, even not said aloud, had no place here. Not when she did this of her own free will. As weird as it seemed, she wanted to do this. Would do this—no matter what.

They walked the full area of the lower floor before Gabe led her back up the stairs and toward the chamber. Already the space around her had filled to double the capacity. Apparently, her impending punishment would be the highlight of the night.

Gabe stopped in front of the glass door of the chamber and waited. In mere seconds the curtains on each side parted, and the surrounding area became illuminated in a soft green glow. The chamber, as they referred to it, was simply a big glass box in one corner of the dungeon play space. When the velvet drapes parted, the other three glass sides were revealed.

Gabe threw her a one-last-chance glance before he turned back and opened the door. He detached her leash and handed it off to one of the many attendants hovering, just waiting to do someone's bidding. Another one of the items she could have pulled from the punishment box.

This time he grabbed her hand and tugged her gently into the center of the room and in the direction of the forced-orgasm tower. Jennifer bit her lip and glanced around her. Once inside, she realized it wasn't nearly as big as it looked from the outside. Gabe turned to her, brushed the hair from her face and planted a chaste kiss on her cheek. "Have fun."

He left the room and two male attendants rushed in, one carrying leather shackles and the other a wicked sneer and an industrial-size wand vibrator. Jennifer hesitated to look beyond the two men. If she saw the intense stares of the crowd along with Daegan glaring at her, she might not be able to hold it together.

One of the men proceeded to attach the soft-as-butter leather cuffs to her wrists. "Raise you arms, sub," he gruffly ordered.

She did while looking up at the wide bar he'd attach her to. In the meantime the second man had nudged her legs apart and wrapped leather around her ankles, attaching her to the base of the tower that served a spreader bar that would keep her legs spread wide no matter what she did. Her arms were then fastened about shoulder-width apart to the metal rod hanging down from the ceiling. Her mobility was quickly diminishing.

The T-rod attachment on the spreader bar had an insert for the vibrator which would then be locked in place against her pussy. Once the toy was in place, Jennifer would have no escape from the constant torment of the device. She could neither remove it nor move away from it for as long as the time on the count-down clock ran. Hence the torture part. She inwardly groaned at that fun thought.

The men began to pinch and fondle her nipples. The chamber was all about extreme arousal and no choice. Despite her thoughts to stay calm throughout the ordeal, a flash of heat began to build in her pussy. One man strayed to the vibrator and hovered, awaiting the signal to go.

"Fifteen minutes on the clock." The crowd cheered, and the switch was flipped. The steady rhythmic buzz of the vibrator directly on top of her clit made Jennifer jerk against her restraints. Her eyes grew wide. Damn she'd forgotten how fucking powerful these things were. Jennifer squeezed her eyes shut against the already tantalizing sensations. She didn't have to do this, she could end it—she wanted to finish. Although the less she had to look into Daegan's eyes while she did, the better.

Teeth scraped at her nipples, sending delicious shards of pleasure straight to her pussy. The added bit of pain made it all the more impossible to resist. Her eyes rolled back in her head as the heat built unbearably high. She wiggled, trying to find a spot of relief to no avail. The contraption allowed her some movement side to side but not enough to get very far or make a damn bit of difference. A moan slipped from her mouth.

Gabe, or whoever remained in charge, must have been satisfied with her response. The men halted their attention. She whimpered—in relief or protest she wasn't sure. She peered out from hooded eyes to see that indeed the men had left her side. She lifted her head to look for Daegan, and the lights winked out. Her adrenaline spiked, a natural response to the sudden change in the scene. She pulled on the restraints over her head and only managed to ignite the fire already simmering between her legs. She cried out.

Murmurs from the crowd were all she heard, reminding her that she was still surrounded by people even though she couldn't see a damn thing.

Just as suddenly as they'd gone out, the lights came

back on. She screamed. Standing not two feet in front of her was a huge, hulking man she'd never seen before. Long dark hair, chiseled jaw, brown eyes that reminded her of melted chocolate...

The quiet of the crowd fractured amid a flurry of whispers, and Daegan stood to the side, a mixture of awe and fury burning through him.

"Who—" Jennifer began to ask.

The man covered her mouth. "You do not have permission to speak, sub." The deep tone of his voice rumbled through the room.

Jennifer clamped her mouth shut, and the stranger began to move around her. Daegan didn't know what the hell was going on, but he didn't like it. Someone, Gabe likely, had changed the game and this new person was about to lay hands on Jennifer.

He started forward, and a Dom he'd talked to a few times in the past held him back. "Her plea to do this for you was very heartfelt. Stopping the scene now could be worse than letting her finish."

Daegan didn't want to hear it. She belonged to him.

He scrubbed his hands across his face. Did she really? She'd fought him every step of the way. Tonight had been the last straw. So why was he going through this with her? Because he didn't want to get suspended for a couple of weeks? Big fucking deal.

"Why do you want this, little sub?" The hulking stranger wrapped his hand around the back of her slim neck and pushed her forward.

She gasped at the slight movement. "Because I broke club rules tonight, Sir."

He smacked her ass. "That's not what I meant and you know it. Look at your Dom and tell him why you want this," he ordered.

Daegan spotted the tear before it slid down her cheek. "Because I was a stupid fool."

The Dom chuckled, his hand moving to her breast. Much more of this, and Daegan feared he'd explode. He never should have allowed her to go through with this.

"What else?"

The question startled him. Who the hell was this man, and why was he dragging this out?

She began to tremble. "I may not understand love, but I want to learn." She turned and looked at him, her body shaking under the onslaught of the vibrations. "And I want my Master to teach me."

For a second Daegan's world tilted. She'd called him

Master. Not Sir. Not by his name. He sucked in a breath.

"Stop." The word came out before he had time to think about it.

Gabe stepped forward. "Daegan, you can't—"

"The fuck I can't. She's mine, and I'm taking her home." Over Gabe's shoulder he saw her shoulders slump in relief.

"About fucking time."

Daegan nailed Gabe with a sharp look. "What did you say?"

"You heard me." He patted him on the shoulder. "Go collect your sub and take her home. I'll see you in a couple of weeks."

Annoyed by the smirk on his friend's face, Daegan moved to Jennifer and unhooked the bindings holding her arms upright while the other man moved to unhook the spreader bar and the attached toy. Freed, she slumped into his arms. "It's okay, love. I've got you." He wanted to simply hold her and help her through whatever tumultuous emotions ran through her, but first he needed to get her out of here.

One of the free assistants came running up with a blanket, and Daegan bundled his contrary sub in the soft fabric. She burrowed against his chest, a move that pierced directly through his heart. He worried how easily she could have been broken if he'd let the punishment continue. Despite her profession and bravado, she simply wasn't ready for that experience.

He made his way through the throngs of people amid more than a few curious stares and whispers. Outside at his car, Daegan opened the rear door and climbed in without letting go of Jennifer. As much as she needed the comfort, so did he.

After a few minutes of silence, Jennifer pulled back and looked up at him. "I'm so sorry."

"For what?" He didn't know where to begin with the things that had gone wrong.

"I'm a total fuckup."

He reached over and pushed the hair out of her eyes. "Fuckup might be a little strong. But you do have some issues with opening up. You keep things so bottled up it's bound to cause problems."

"I tried to tell you..."

"And I didn't listen. Is that what you're saying?" he sighed. His temper flared. "You made a choice to come here. I think I got the message loud and clear, Jennifer."

"This is exactly why I stick so rigidly to a routine. Work, exercise, meals, and sleep. Every fucking time I step outside those parameters, things go to shit. I'm not cut out for anything else."

"Stop. This self-indulgent woe-is-me thinking is exactly what got you into trouble tonight. You think I don't know what's best for you? Really?"

"I don't even know what's best for me right now, how can you?"

White-hot anger flooded through him. What she fucking needed was the spanking of her life. He grabbed her around the waist and flipped her over. The blanket fell away, leaving her naked and vulnerable on his lap. Good.

"I have never met a sub who needed frequent and regular centering more than you do." He delivered the first blow dead center on her right cheek. The smack of his hand hitting flesh pumped satisfaction through his body. She jerked against him but didn't try to squirm away or protest.

"When your life veers off course, you panic. Somewhere along the way, you've discovered that a painful flogging can clear your mind. What you don't yet understand is that the indifference afterward has a lingering effect. That kind of impersonal approach isn't a long-term solution." He delivered another hard, stinging blow. The first sob tore through her. He spanked her again, setting up a rough and steady rhythm across the fleshy skin of her bottom and the tops of her thighs. Pink turned to red, and he imagined the heat burning through her by now.

After a few minutes, he paused to check her breathing and caress the inflamed skin of her cheeks. Her sobs grew rougher, and the wet tears seeped into his pants.

"I'm so sorry," she wailed.

He shook his head and began spanking her again. This wasn't about him; it was her. She had to get it all out once and for all. He wished he'd had the patience to wait till they'd returned home. A nice thick paddle or even a vicious little switch would be perfect right about now. He wanted to stripe her ass and leave her so sore that every time she sat down for the next two days, she'd think of what he'd done for her. He quickened his pace, making sure he hit with a precision that would sting, sending jolts of pain outward.

Minutes later, he sensed the change. Her body shook under the onslaught of full body-racking sobs. The kind born from deeply repressed emotions pent-up over long periods of time. His heart broke a little with each rough shudder, but this was what she'd needed. This catharsis to freedom.

When it was done, he caressed the red-hot skin for a long time while her sobs died down to small hiccups. "It's all right, sweetheart," he cooed. He bent to bury his face in her hair and hold her as close as he could. His fingers traced the length of her arm and back again in a slow hypnotic pattern. When her breathing evened, he pushed his fingers between her thighs and along her wet slit. He throbbed for her, but he wasn't going to do this now. He'd take her home first and take care of her. Tuck her into bed, and then he'd fuck her.

And he did. Later as they lay twined together in the tiny bed of his guest bedroom, he relived the events of their night. The progress she'd made when pushed astounded him. Unfortunately, he had real doubts about her ability to move past this point and develop into a deeper relationship. And like it or not, that's where they were headed.

He ran his fingers through her soft hair, the need to touch her almost constant. Her breathing slowed as she faded into sleep. "You still drive me crazy," he whispered into the night. "I'm just not sure that's enough with your past still hanging over you."

"What?"

Shit. She was still awake. "Sorry, love. I was just thinking out loud." He saw the instant his meaning clicked, and her mouth opened to say something he was sure he wouldn't like. He grabbed her by the shoulders and kissed her. After a few tense seconds, she relaxed into his embrace and some of the anxiety between them faded. He moved his lips over hers in a soft caress. Between anger and sadness, her body still responded to his cues. He wrapped his hand around her neck and held her still while he continued his erotic assault. When he finally pulled away, it only took one look to see she was now putty in his hands.

"Deny all you want, love. This ends tonight one way or the other."

CHAPTER 15

*J*ennifer walked into Altered Ego on Monday morning as if nothing had happened. At least as far as outward appearances went. Inside, her stomach threatened to revolt every few minutes. Why did she insist on dwelling on the bullshit? After the most amazing night of her life, she'd let insecurity come between them one last time when he'd expressed his concerns about her ability to make a long-term commitment, and it had been the last straw. Not that she'd waited around for him to cool down.

They'd had a simple agreement. Temporary. Instead she'd fallen for him hard. Weeks of buildup between them had resulted in an explosive few days that she couldn't get out of her mind. All weekend, she'd secretly harbored these ridiculous fantasies of her knight in shining armor coming to her door to rescue her. Or at least trying to salvage their relationship. No dice.

The door opened behind her, and she braced herself for Eve's Monday morning excitement.

"Are you okay?"

She jumped at the deep tone of Chase's voice. Since when did her boss show up at the studio this early? That's just what she needed. She wasn't quite ready to fake happiness with Eve, let alone a man who had an uncanny ability to see far beyond the surface. *Too bad, so sad.* She stood up straight and took several deep breaths.

"Doing great. How are you?" To her credit, her voice didn't waver.

Chase said nothing, and the silence stretched between them. She fought the urge to look over her shoulder and see if he still stood there. It didn't matter; she knew he did. There were times the man had an amazing amount of patience. Like when he waited for the perfect shot. Sometimes instead of taking one thousand pictures during a shoot, he'd watch and wait. Her body would cramp, sweat would bead across her brow, and still he'd wait. On days like that, after eight hours of work there might only be a dozen or so pictures, but each and every single one of them would be amazing.

Unable to withstand the pressure of his stare at her back, she turned. As she'd expected, he scrutinized her closely from his comfortable position of leaning against the wall. "Is that so?"

It sounded like a question, but she didn't think it was. Still she shrugged.

"Ready to come back to work?"

It didn't take a rocket scientist to know he meant modeling. For so long it had meant the world to her to be the best damn fetish model in the business. She'd worked hard over the years, training and building up her endurance. Until Daegan had come along, she'd had her schedule filled with jobs and had been damn happy about it. She'd been right to call him the devil. The man came in like a whirlwind and turned her life upside down and shook everything loose.

At first she'd resented the way her body responded to him. He made her feel out of control, and it scared her. Although, somewhere along the line, her world changed. She'd planned to tell Chase she was ready to work again; instead, in that moment her future became crystal clear.

"No."

His eyebrows arched in question.

"I think it's time for me to move on from modeling."

Chase pushed off the wall and crossed the room. He cupped her chin and tilted her head until their gazes met. "I had a feeling you'd say that."

"You did?"

He laughed, releasing her. "Of course. I knew the minute you got a taste of something real, modeling would never be the same for you."

"You say that like it's a bad thing."

"Not at all. You were a damn near perfect model, Jennifer, but your heart needed something else. Someone else."

She smiled at his assessment. "No. It's not about someone else. It's about me. I've spent my entire life hiding with my clothes off. I don't want to hide anymore. Daegan may not love me back, but he taught me that it's possible."

The corners of Chase's mouth quirked in an almost smile. "Love, huh? I expected as much. And Eve damn well drove us mad with her insistence on the matter."

Jennifer cringed. Had she really let the love word slip? What an idiot. "I—uhh—I—"

"Don't be afraid of it, little rabbit. You can run, but it'll get you eventually. Trust me. Now what are you going to do about it?" he asked.

"There's nothing to be done. I screwed up, and even my attempt to fix things went sour. I think it's time to start something new with a clean slate."

"You are nothing like her, you know."

Jennifer froze, a sudden chill sweeping over her. She didn't have to ask; she knew exactly who Chase meant.

"The physical resemblance is minimal. Every once in a while when I catch you in the right light, I think you look like her. Any other time the thought doesn't even cross my mind."

A slight tremble shook through her. "Please don't." She didn't want to talk about Daegan's dead wife anymore. The whole situation had gotten blown out of proportion, she knew, yet she'd allowed the niggling at the back of her brain to ruin everything.

Chase continued, "Beyond that. It's like seeing the difference between night and day. Claire was a selfish woman who took advantage of every opportunity she could."

"That sounds like personal knowledge."

"We were all in college together. Daegan asked her out the night he met her, and Claire, well, she didn't think he was good enough for her, so she turned him down. Until she found out about the money."

Jennifer blinked. "The money?"

Chase paused. "Daegan didn't tell you?"

She shook her head.

"He inherited a huge fortune from his father just before we started college. Said fortune came with everything his family owned for generations, including a castle in Ireland."

Jennifer's eyes widened at the thought.

"Yeah, so he started dating Claire, and one thing led to another, and before he could see through her, it was too late; they were married."

She didn't think she wanted to hear more details. Leaving him behind was hard enough without any more information. "I don't think I need to know this," she insisted.

"Of course you do. Part of your problem with Daegan is that you think he looks at you and sees her. You need to trust that he doesn't." He paused and let that sink in. "Right after they got married, they began to experiment in D/s, and before long, they were heavily involved. Only Claire needed more than Daegan ever wanted to give. But she was his wife, and a Dom's responsibility is to give his sub what she needs. So he allowed her to evolve into a 24-7 slave. She expected Daegan to direct every moment of her day and then some."

Jennifer shuddered. She admired many a couple who managed that type of relationship, but no way in hell could she go for that. "I could never—I mean—why would he want that from me?"

"You're missing the point I'm trying to make. That's exactly what he doesn't want. But just because you can't be a slave master doesn't mean you can live without the whole thing. He is a Dom. He needs a sub, and you are the one he wants."

She violently shook her head. "You're wrong. He thinks I'm broken." She didn't know how to let go of the emotions ripping through her.

"Honey, you're not broken. A little misguided, sure. Broken? No. Deep down you know exactly what you want. Otherwise you wouldn't be here telling me you aren't going to model anymore. As soon as you stop trying to analyze the relationship, you'll figure out how to make it work."

"But—"

Chase placed a finger across her lips to quiet her. "No more buts. Use that brain to come up with a solution. Do something unexpected." He glanced around the room. "Now where's my Eve? I need something from her this morning." Chase winked and wandered away, leaving her stunned.

Could he be right? She'd waited all weekend for him to

come for her and got nothing. Did she dare reach out to him one more time? The submission she'd felt in the club and afterward had burned into her soul, never to be forgotten. What wouldn't she do for an opportunity to feel that again?

She missed him...

Maybe there were two devils in this playground.

LATER THAT AFTERNOON, Jennifer slipped into Daegan's quiet apartment. The scent of his skin assailed her senses. Wood and spice flooded her thoughts. No matter what happened, she'd forever associate those two smells with her week as Daegan's submissive. Her stomach knotted at the thought of only having those short memories to keep her company at night, instead of the real man. She glanced at the clock and calculated she had an hour tops before he arrived. The guest bedroom door had been closed, and she felt the lead weight of that statement. He'd closed her room. She ignored the finality of that gesture and hurried into his office.

She took a seat in front of the computer. After she powered it up, she navigated to her blog and began her next entry. A couple of years ago, she'd started blogging about her adventures as a fetish model, and she'd taken

E.M. GAYLE

to the online journaling of her thoughts like a fish to water. Albeit not her more intimate thoughts. Now she'd have to change things up. She'd no longer be modeling, instead she had an all-new subject to blog about. She settled in to start.

For years I have come here and chronicled some of my experiences as a fetish model. You've learned firsthand about the complexities that go into a photo shoot and seen some of the more "real" photos. Unfortunately or fortunately, depending on how you look at it, this blog has to change. I know this is going to come as a surprise to many of you, but you should know that I didn't come to this decision lightly. I am officially retiring from modeling, effective immediately.

Now before you start sending me your comments and asking me if I'm crazy, you should know this. Nothing bad happened that made me come to this decision. I still love modeling and am going to be forever grateful to Chase and Murphy at Altered Ego for giving me the big break I needed.

But my life has changed.

A week ago, I agreed to become someone's submissive. I took a step out of my safety zone that had far-reaching repercussions. Who at this point doesn't matter for the purpose of this blog. What matters is the what and the why in the outcome. You see, I thought I was simply indulging a fantasy. A temporary arrangement that would get it out of my system. Oh how wrong I was.

Jennifer's fingers flew over the keyboard as she poured her heart and soul into this blog post. With every sentence, more of what she'd experienced began to click inside her. Before she knew it, she'd written about three thousand words. She'd have to break this up into a series. She cut and pasted it into three documents and scheduled three different posts to go live over the next couple of weeks. With any luck, she'd be too busy to check her blog daily.

Time was running close. She quickly logged into her e-mail and pasted the link in an e-mail to text message. Daegan kept his CrackBerry at his side at all times, so if there was any way to get him to see this, this would be it. Her finger hovered over the Send button. *Please work. Please work. Please work.* She pressed the key and gulped for air. Her heart rate soared. Now the wait of her life would begin. There was nothing more she could do except get ready for his arrival.

The next part of her plan didn't exactly qualify as "crazy" as Chase had put it, but it was her best shot at effective. The blog post was daring, this was simply a gesture that had deep meaning for her.

She hurried into her bedroom and stripped. A flutter of nerves made her hesitate. The last time she'd done this, it had gone very wrong when someone other than Daegan had found her. Jennifer shrugged. It was simply a chance she had to take. She climbed into the bed and stuck her face in the pillow next to hers. She wanted to bottle that scent. If she did, she'd make a million bucks in a heartbeat.

Like before, she cuffed one wrist and checked the rope to be certain it was secured to the bedpost. Satisfied with her plan thus far, she snuggled into the comforter to wait. And hope.

CHAPTER 16

Daegan sipped at his coffee while watching the sun set through his office window. It had been a busy but productive day. While they still had a long way to go to project completion, they were getting close to opening the second phase. Once a few of the shops opened, there would be a lot more foot traffic through the building, and he'd have to ensure the guests were disturbed as little as possible by his crews. He glanced at his watch. All of his contractors would have left the site by now, leaving not much reason for him to stay. His foul mood when he'd arrived had spurred him into action, and he'd tackled the mountain of paperwork awaiting his attention. Caught up with work, he could head home and... And what?

Spend another night with his best friend Jack getting sloppy drunk again. He shook his head. No, he and

Jack Daniels needed to go on a break. Jennifer on the other hand was a different story entirely. As soon as the door had closed behind her on Friday night, his regrets had begun. His head told him one thing, while his heart and body said another. He'd fought the impulse to drag her back inside and tie her to the wall.

He couldn't get her off his mind though, so he'd avoided the photo studio and shops all day long. Now that everyone had left the building, he could do a quick sweep through the first floor and make sure the last of the adjustments were complete.

The phone on his hip buzzed with an incoming text. Good. Maybe he'd find something there to keep his mind occupied. Then he saw the incoming message came from Jennifer. Surprised she'd made contract, he pressed the few buttons to make her message pop up.

Please read. It's important.

Hmm. What was his sub up to? No, not his.

He clicked on the link, and the Web browser popped up and navigated to a blog called Submissive in the South. Intrigued, he started to read.

His jaw dropped when he got to the part about her retiring from modeling. What? He sat up straight. She had his attention now. He continued on.

My new Dom doled out some rules that I was to abide

by, and my very first thought was hell no. But I had agreed to try, and after the night we'd spent together, any denial at that point would have been an obvious lie. It wasn't just my body that loved everything he put me through. My mind did as well. Something began to slowly unravel inside me. I wish I could have easily accepted the changes my heart urged me to make, but years of living alone with only myself to rely on had taken their toll.

What you don't know about me and what I didn't understand either was the time I spent at the local BDSM club had reasoning behind it. I used to spend all of my time and energy focused on work. I was either at a shoot, training for a shoot, studying for a shoot or resting in preparation of a shoot. Most of the time that narrow focus worked great. Although, every couple of months I would grow irritable and restless. It's as if my mind had an autopilot mechanism that said enough is enough. I was so frustrated with myself I didn't know what to do, so off I'd go to the club to allow some stranger to beat it out of me with his flogger.

This cycle worked for me, or so I thought.

Now I know better.

For now, I leave you with this thought, and next post I will continue the story of how I became a submissive.

So many of us come from less than perfect backgrounds. Some with love and some without. One thing I've learned over the years that has now become perfectly clear—We do not have to be defined by our past. Who we are comes from what we choose to do now in the present. I've chosen to be honest.

Daegan stared at the words, hardly able to absorb them. Did his little sub really just admit to the whole world, or anyone who potentially read her blog, the mistakes of her past and present?

He got up and strode to the window, searching for her car. When he spied the dark blue vehicle in its regular spot—hope soared. His Jennifer was still in the building, and he had an idea where he might find her. Blood tinged with excitement surged through his veins as he took the stairs two at a time to get to her.

Daegan opened the door to his apartment and prayed he was right. He practically ran to the spare bedroom, only slowing his steps moments before he walked through the door.

Sure enough, his beautiful sub had cuffed herself to his bed once again. This time though, they were going to do things right. Everything he'd thought he didn't need came to him wrapped in the perfect Jennifer package. Challenges and all.

"Jennifer."

"Yes, Sir?"

He lowered his voice, "Take off the cuff and come here. Now."

She slowly turned to do as he asked with a shaky hand. Once freed, she hesitated as if reluctant, before she got up from the bed and stood before him. "I'm sorry. I only thought—"

"I know what you thought." He admired her lovely body. Under his perusal, her eyes went dark, and he imagined the wetness growing between her thighs.

He wanted her so badly he ached. Only the memory of her defiance and denial kept him thinking logically. Daegan grappled for control, cupped her chin, and lifted her face. "I think you do too much thinking. In fact, I've been far too lenient with you to this point."

She wisely kept her mouth shut, only bringing her tongue out briefly to lick her lips. He enjoyed that small show of nerves. Keeping her off-balance would be his new favorite goal.

"Are you really ready to commit to our arrangement this time?"

She bowed her head, her beautiful hair obscuring part of her face. His cock jerked at the submissive move.

"I want nothing more than to put my full trust and

faith in you." She hesitated for only a second. "Master."

"I won't deny I like the sound of that when you say it. But giving over to me isn't just physical. We'll grow together emotionally. This isn't club play."

"I already have," she whispered. "I don't know where that's headed or if it's something I can even do long-term, but I know I want to try."

Daegan's heart pounded against his ribs. He'd never truly considered another permanent relationship could be in the cards for him. While he and Jennifer still had a hell of a lot of road to cover, he now had hope.

"Afraid, are you?" He released her chin and wrapped his hand around the back of her neck, squeezing with a firm grip.

"Nervous," she mumbled.

"Like I said before, I've been too lenient. Don't expect me to go easy anymore."

She nodded. "I understand, Master."

His body leaped to life every time she called him that. He didn't doubt between the punishment scene at the club and the spanking afterward in the car, something had clicked inside her. They'd both been life-altering moments for him as well. First her sacrifice and then her breakdown. Walking away from that had been the hardest thing he'd ever done.

"Come with me." Using his hand tight on her neck, he steered her out of the small spare bedroom and into his personal space. He'd guarded her those first nights from some of his more extreme tastes until she grew used to him. Tonight, that hesitation ended.

He flipped a panel of switches, and the room flooded with light. While his eyes attempted to adjust to the sudden change, Jennifer gasped. Obviously, she'd gotten her first eyeful of the Dark Room he'd begun transforming into a personal dungeon space in preparation for his new penthouse.

"This is all yours, Master?"

He turned her into his arms and banded them around her. In the bright spotlights he'd installed, her skin paled to the color of fine porcelain china, from the curve of her shoulders to the slopes of her breasts flattened against his chest. His breath hitched. He wanted to make sure he saw every shade of pink and every mark her body took from him.

"I've had a little time on my hands these past months and making these things kept my frustration at bay." Some items were simple, such as the St. Andrew's cross attached to the wall and the leather padded spanking bench next to it. Along the edge of the cross he'd attached screw bolts and hung his new collection of floggers and whips. Even the cage in the corner he'd handcrafted after hours when the building stood practically empty.

However, his favorite piece had to be the bed. Its four thick bedposts joined to the wooden frame canopy gave it an old-world feel compared to today's more modern lightweight furniture. Of course, what looked innocent enough was easily transformed with the special fittings he'd installed for slings, mirrors, stocks, and a wide variety of restraint options.

"Before the night is over, every inch of you will be explored, used, and fucked. Now go get on the bed, lie on your back, and spread your legs wide for me, love."

The slight tremble that shook through her brought a smile to his face. To her credit, she did his bidding without hesitation. She looked fucking gorgeous on his bed, turning his masterpiece into a true work of art. It took more than a little restraint on his part not to fall on top of her and fuck like a madman.

"Lift your arms over your head, love."

Again, she complied. He grabbed a pair of leather cuffs and a bottle of lubricant from the cubby at the end of the bed and moved next to her, sliding against the heated smooth skin of her thigh. He ignored the need to take her fast, quickly strapping the cuffs to her wrists before attaching them to the eyebolts at the top of the bed. Needing to ensure he'd made the proper fit, he slid his fingers under her cuffs to check circulation. Satisfied with his work, he turned his attention to the naked sub in his bed. His sub.

Determined to take it slow, he planned to inspect all of her sweet spots. He slid between her legs, bracing himself on his forearms between her thighs. The bare flesh of her pussy already glistened with her arousal, the soft scent filtering through his mind. Reaching out, he spread her labia to get a better look. Her clit looked puffy, partially protruding from the hood that covered it. He brushed a finger across the tiny bundle of nerves and was rewarded with a sharp intake of breath.

Desire coiled tight in his belly at the amazing picture she presented. He needed to do something quick before he went mad and thrust into her like an animal. What could he say? She had that kind of effect on his control.

Daegan leaned forward and blew air across her wet flesh. Her tremble started low and traveled up her body, followed by the red flush of her skin. Damn, but that was hot. He swiped his tongue along her folds, up one side and down the other, allowing the taste of her to sink into his head. When her legs jerked, he grabbed her thighs and held them down. He wanted to take his time and imprint this moment on his memory forever.

Her, here, in his bed for the first time. He circled her clit, being careful not to touch it quite yet. Didn't want her going off too soon. He licked and coaxed and scraped with his teeth until he was rewarded with a fully revealed swollen kernel of flesh begging for his attention.

Her breathing grew erratic, peppered with small and longer drawn-out moans that went straight to his head. She arched her hips, and he lifted his head. "Be still or I'll stop," he warned.

She whimpered before relaxing into the mattress. "Good girl," he cooed. "No matter what you do, there won't be an orgasm until I say so. If you don't behave, there's a good chance you won't get one. Am I clear?"

She bit her bottom lip and nodded her head. "Yes, Sir," she finally answered breathlessly.

"I haven't had dinner yet, and I'm starved." He bent again to her cunt and lapped hungrily at the wet flesh. He had every intention of bringing her to the edge over and over again until she melted in front of him in a helpless beg.

He spied her pulling on his restraints and took that opportunity to suck her clit between his lips, worrying it with his teeth. She tossed her head and cried out but somehow managed to do as he'd asked and remain still. Time to up the stakes.

He plunged two fingers inside her, brushing against all the nerve endings guaranteed to light her up like a Christmas tree. Her muscles flexed and clenched on his fingers, and he nearly lost his own mind at the sensation. He wanted to feel that around his dick.

Damn...

Her skin heated and flushed a deep red, her labia swelled, and her clit turned hard. She couldn't fight it much longer without losing it. He felt her clamp down in a feeble attempt to stop the rising orgasm. He opted to give her a brief respite and pulled away from the delicious pussy he couldn't get enough of. He stood at the edge of the bed and watched her regain control. A sheen of perspiration covered her lovely skin, and the telltale twitching of muscles in her thighs gave her struggle away.

He wasn't done challenging her. He bit back the smile of satisfaction creeping through him. With his gaze locked to her flushed face, he slapped the pad of her pussy, ensuring the force of his swat reverberated through her clit.

Jennifer cried out, thrashed against her restraints. He repeated the process, each time watching her reaction to the pain that turned to pleasure. Her eyes dilated, the sounds coming from her mouth guttural, while the sensations overwhelmed her. She was quickly tumbling into subspace.

Daegan halted the blows and ignored the whimpers of her protest. He once again slid two fingers inside her, noticing the marked increase in moisture. She'd obviously enjoyed the pussy spanking. So had he. He added another finger and stretched her wide with ease. "Remember what I said about remaining still?"

She slowly nodded her head. She was floating but still aware. He added a generous amount of liquid to his hand and worked it in gently with each inward push.

"That's about to become very important. Take a few deep breaths and relax for me." She followed his instructions, and he felt the muscles clamping his fingers loosen. "That's right, keep breathing." Inside her he made slow circles with his hand, applying gentle pressure outward, opening her before he slipped a fourth finger inside along the other three.

"Are you..." The question came out slightly slurred.

"Yes. So stay relaxed." He now watched her expressions like a hawk, looking for the slightest indication he was pushing her too far. He continued a slow massage of her pretty pink cunt until her mewls turned to cries and pure rapture crossed her face. "Breathe, love." He pushed gently until his whole hand filled her. She gasped and shook, her thighs spreading wider. His own head buzzed at the incredible sight before him. He remained still, letting her drive the motions for now.

She writhed around on his hand, drawing closer to the inevitable orgasm.

He wiggled his fingers. "Come now, love. Come for me sweetheart." Her body tightened around him and a scream pealed through the room, rendering him utterly speechless at the pure beauty of her submission.

The force of her contractions caught him off guard, leaving him gasping for air. He'd never experienced such a fierce orgasm from a sub. Amazed and feeling in awe, he pulled gently out of her. He disappeared into the bathroom to clean up and regain a modicum of control. His cock throbbed worse than an aching tooth, driving him mad. He stripped his clothes and left them lying on the bathroom floor and returned to her.

Harsh breathing filled the room. Neither had recovered. He massaged her legs from ankles to hip until she'd relaxed and her breathing returned to normal. He couldn't hold off from taking her much longer. Jennifer had turned out to be the woman of his fantasies, and she'd burrowed under his skin from the get-go. Suddenly eager to take her further, he flipped her onto her stomach, crossing her arms over her head and pushing her knees underneath her to lift her ass.

With jerky motions, born of unmet need, he palmed her ass and spread her cheeks. One look at the pink rosette, and his control broke like a dried-out twig. He reached behind him for the bottle of lubricant and squeezed a large dollop to the tiny hole. With one finger he worked the liquid inside her until she moaned underneath him. Damn, but she responded like a dream to everything he wanted. "Do you have any idea how much I've been dying to fuck you here?"

She half moaned, half whined in response. His heart clenched. If he wasn't already half in love with this woman, he'd have fallen tonight. She'd embraced her submission and come to him of her own free will and then some. That meant more to him than she could imagine.

"Take me, Master. Please." Her husky plea sent blood roaring through his veins. Who was he to deny her now?

He fitted the head of his cock to her tight hole and began a slow slide inside her. At the tight ring he paused. "You take me, little sub. Show me how much you want my cock in your tight ass."

She didn't hesitate; she pushed down and back. With her temporarily controlling the moves, the resistance gave way with little effort, and he found himself balls-deep in a tight fist of molten heat. He gripped her hips, digging in to keep from plowing into her. When her body adjusted, she began to wiggle on him. He drew back, then plunged in with a hungry thrust. Not once, over and over again. One deep push after another as their bodies melded together in the rhythm of two people who desperately needed each other. From ugly pasts they were being given a second chance—something he had no intention of giving up on.

His body tensed, pushing him closer to his own edge of release with each plunge into her welcoming body. He didn't want to go by himself, so he reached around and thumbed her clit. Jennifer cried out, her body tightening around him to the point of overload.

"Come for me, love. One more time. Come," he commanded.

She shuddered and thrashed harder—sending him headlong into the point of no return as his climax crashed over him. He groaned, thrusting deep, lifting her knees right off the bed he hammered so hard, emptying inside her sweet, sweet ass.

When his thoughts cleared, he eased his grip and lowered her back to the bed. He withdrew, massaging her ass and thighs. Daegan mustered the energy to lean forward and release her cuffs before he collapsed on the bed beside her. He'd carry them to the shower in a minute. Right now his legs felt like wet noodles.

He brushed the silky strands from Jennifer's upturned face. "Are you okay?"

She mumbled some response before sinking into the arms he wrapped around her. His little sub needed recovery time. Some amount of time passed as they both drifted in and out of sleep. When he opened his eyes again, he found her beautiful baby blues staring back at him. He had a feeling she was waiting for him to say something.

"That was an incredible gift, love. You pleased me very much." He rubbed his hand slowly up and down her spine. "Your text message turned into the surprise of my life."

A slow smile spread across her face, as did a rosy blush. "It's the only thing I could think of to show you how much of an impact you made on me."

He looked around the room at his various toys. "Oh I can think of many other ways."

She rolled her eyes, and he tapped her on her butt in retaliation. "It was a beautiful gesture, but I think we need a new agreement."

She blinked up at him. "We do?"

"Mmm hmm." He nuzzled her neck. "If you're going to be my submissive to do with as I please, I think we'll need some new rules."

She blanched. "More rules? Don't we have enough?"

"Just one. But it's the hardest one of all." He reached between them to rub her already bunched nipples. "No more running."

She opened her mouth to say something. He narrowed his gaze and pressed two fingers to her lips. "Say it."

Her breath hitched before she spoke. "No more running," she repeated.

"Good girl. Because next time... I'm not letting you go."

A smile curled her lips, lust and love shining in her eyes. "Thank you, Master."

* * *

Thank you so much for reading!

If you enjoyed this book please take a moment to help other readers discover it by leaving a review on your favorite retailer.

Just a few words and some stars really does help!

CAUGHT up on the *Pleasure Playground* series and

want more like it? Then keep reading for the BONUS EXCERPT from **TUCKER'S FALL!**

Join Eliza's VIP newsletter at emgayle.com/news and be the first to be notified of new releases, sales and contests.

If you're on Facebook or Twitter, come by and say hello! I'd love to hear from you.

Continue reading for a bonus excerpt from TUCKER'S FALL , the first book in the Purgatory Masters series and the full booklist from E.M. Gayle.

ABOUT TUCKER'S FALL

TUCKER'S FALL

By
E.M. Gayle
Copyright 2013

Scandalized professor Maggie Cisco returns to her hometown to lick her wounds and reconsider her future. Her years of research into the BDSM lifestyle has landed her in jail, in divorce court and now in the headlines of more newspapers than she cares to count. The worst of all? The entire debacle is being blamed on a bestselling book she hasn't even read!

Just when she thinks her only solution is a tell all memoir, a snowstorm puts her in the path of stunningly handsome, insanely rich and equally intense, Tucker Lewis.

Tucker remembers Maggie well. They once shared a mind-numbing kiss at the annual St. Mary's carnival when her boyfriend wasn't looking. No stranger to scandal, he looks past public opinion to the submissive craving a master's touch and decides then and there what he wants. He's going after Maggie and her heart's kinkiest desires.

Unfortunately, no amount of money can change the sins of the past and when they're certain they know everything there is to know about each other, one discovers a secret they aren't prepared for.

Tucker's Fall is the first book in a new series called **Purgatory Masters**. This is a spinoff from the Purgatory Club series that includes Roped, Watch Me, Teased, Burn, Bottoms Up and Hold Me Close. You do not have to read the Purgatory Club series first to enjoy Tucker's Fall, but once you experience Purgatory you might want to read them all.

TUCKER'S FALL BONUS

EXCERPT

ucker Lewis stared into the crowd and wondered when it would all end. He tightened his grip on the shot of Jameson and brought the glass to his lips. Across the bar and generous play space, fake smoke, dancers in chains, and throngs of half-naked partiers filled the club. The intense edge of the Lords of Acid music and the occasional scream of a submissive from the far side of the room fit right in with his dark mood. For better or worse this was the place he'd needed to be tonight.

The Purgatory club had come to be in a different life for him and the longer he sat here watching the scene around him; the less he believed he belonged. Of course his self-imposed exile hadn't helped much. He'd been riding high on life on borrowed time and didn't even know it. All it took was a simple house fire to bring his world crashing down.

"Wow, as I live and breath. Is that you, Tuck?"

Yanked from his mournful thoughts, Tucker focused on the man standing in front of him. Tall and imposing, he wore black leather that emphasized a gleaming bald-head that drew women of all ages. It didn't surprise him that his old friend from better days and one of the best damn rope riggers on the planet stood there with a smug grin.

"Fuck you, Leo."

"C'mon, Tucker. You know I'm not your type. But maybe this one is." Leo tugged on a leash he'd been holding and a very pretty redhead cautiously stepped out from behind him. Even with her eyes cast down, it didn't take much for Tucker to recognize her nervous-ness. Her hands intertwined with each other repeat-edly as she shifted her weight from foot to foot.

Long, red hair brushed the tops of ample breasts that were barely hidden by a thin, black nightie that stopped before her thighs began. But it was the thick leather collar at her neck, branded with two names that stood out to him.

"I see things have changed for you since I last visited."

"Tends to happen when you disappear from the face of

the Earth." Leo clapped his shoulder and took a seat on the bench next to him and his lovely submissive went to her knees on the floor at Leo's feet.

Tucker tried to ignore the slight pang inside him. It had been a long time since a submissive had caught his eye but that didn't mean the desire to have one of his own had completely disappeared.

"Will you introduce me to your lovely?"

Leo beamed. "Katie, say hello to Master Tucker. He's an old friend of mine."

With what looked like some reluctance, the little subbie lifted her head and met his gaze. "Hello, Master Tucker. It is nice to meet you." Immediately her eyes lowered back to the floor.

"You'll have to excuse Katie this evening. She's had a tough time with her commitments lately so Quinn and I have decided to devote this entire week to her correction." Leo stroked his pet's hair and brushed her cheek when she turned toward him.

The pang inside him clamored louder. The affection between Master and submissive was so obvious it was difficult for Tucker not to experience some degree of jealousy, although settling down had never been in his previous plans. "No need to excuse her. I completely understand." Maybe it was time to get back into the scene. He could meet a willing submissive here at the club and work out some of the kinks that had plagued his art this week.

"You thinking about rejoining us? Maybe some play tonight?"

Tucker shrugged, amazed Leo had read his mind. Tucker's body warred with his mind for control. Part of him definitely needed to move on, but the other—well, he wasn't so sure.

"I'd be happy to offer Katie for service tonight. I think it would do her some good. She needs to get her head in the right place for everything she will be put through this week. What do you say?"

Tucker considered the offer while staring at the top of the pretty sub's head. She'd not uttered a word or made a move except for the tiny shudder he'd detected along her shoulder line when Leo offered her services. She impressed him and that wasn't an easy thing to do these days.

He stood from his seat and positioned himself legs apart in front of Katie. Leaning down he cupped her chin and titled her head back until her gaze met his. "I have a feeling I would enjoy your service very much."

She swallowed before a small smile tilted her lips. Whatever trouble she'd been having it was obvious how much she needed whatever Leo wanted to give her.

"It would be my pleasure, Sir."

A part of him really wanted to enjoy Katie. To take part in her discipline and let go of some of the stress he'd endured lately. His self-imposed exile needed to come to an end. He wasn't his father's son anymore. Unfortunately, his body had a mind of its own and wouldn't cooperate like he wanted it to. Flashes of another lovely lady filled his head. A woman he'd not actually laid eyes on in over fifteen years. Maggie Cisco. Professor. Newly single. Closeted submissive.

While he couldn't actually confirm the submissive part yet, his gut told him the truth. She'd been studying BDSM for so long there was no doubt in his mind there was a hidden ache behind her research. And he refused to entertain the alternative of her being a top. That didn't match the Maggie he knew from high school at all. Sure, people changed. He certainly had, but the fundamental core of who you are and what you need on a cellular level doesn't change in adulthood.

He'd bet every last dollar that Maggie possessed the heart of a true submissive, longing to take her place at her Master's side and he'd waited her out long enough. Her reappearance eight weeks ago had sparked more than gossip. Something inside him akin to hunger had unfurled and dug in with razor sharp claws and refused to let go. His recovery had taken a very long time. Too long. Now he needed to rejoin the world, engage in a healthy if somewhat temporary relationship and he'd chosen Maggie to do it with. She didn't know it yet, but he was coming for her.

Read more now

ALSO BY E.M. GAYLE

Purgatory Masters Series:

TUCKER'S FALL

LEVI'S ULTIMATUM

MASON'S RULE

GABE'S OBSESSION

Purgatory Club:

ROPED

WATCH ME

TEASED

BURN

BOTTOMS UP

HOLD ME CLOSE

Pleasure Playground Series:

PLAY WITH ME

POWER PLAY

Single Title:

SUBMISSIVE BEAUTY

BOOKS WRITING AS ELIZA GAYLE

PARANORMAL ROMANCE

Southern Shifters Series:

DIRTY SEXY FURRY

MATE NIGHT

ALPHA KNOWS BEST

BAD KITTY

BE WERE

SHIFTIN' DIRTY

BEAR NAKED TRUTH

ALPHA BEAST

Devils Point Wolves:

WILD

WICKED

WANTED

FERAL

FIERCE

FURY

Bound by Magick Series:

UNTAMED MAGICK

MAGICK IGNITED

FORCE OF MAGICK

MAGICK PROVOKED

Single titles:

VAMPIRE AWAKENING

ALPHA WOLF RISING

Made in the USA
Coppell, TX
28 March 2022

75678060R00152